Read Aloud Spooky Stories

Cover illustrated by Robin Moro
Title page illustrated by John Manders
Borders illustrated by Jeffrey Ebbeler

Louis Weber, C.E.O.
Publications International, Ltd.
7373 North Cicero Avenue
Lincolnwood, Illinois 60712

Ground Floor, 59 Gloucester Place
London W1U 8JJ

Customer Service: 1-800-595-8484 or customer_service@pilbooks.com

www.pilbooks.com

Manufactured in China.

8 7 6 5 4 3 2 1

ISBN-13: 978-0-7853-6338-5
ISBN-10: 0-7853-6338-6

Read Aloud

Spooky Stories

publications international, ltd.

Table of Contents

Little Orphant Annie

From the original poem by James Whitcomb Riley

Little Orphant Annie's come to our house to stay,
And wash the cups and saucers up, and brush the crumbs away,
And shoo the chickens off the porch, and dust the hearth, and sweep,
And make the fire, and bake the bread, and earn her board-and-keep;
And all us other children, when the supper-things is done,
We sit around the kitchen fire and have the mostest fun,
A-listenin' to the spooky tales that Annie tells about,
And the gobble-uns that will get you
If you
Don't
Watch
Out!

The Canterville Ghost

Based on the original story by Oscar Wilde
Adapted by Renee Deshommes
Illustrated by Stacy Schuett

Mr. Hiram Otis was moving his family to Canterville Chase in England. It was a grand old house and everyone said it was haunted. But Mr. Otis did not agree. "There are no such things as ghosts," he told Lord Canterville.

Lord Canterville described all of the ghostly sightings. But Mr. Otis refused to believe. A few weeks later, he was joined by Mrs. Otis and their four children.

Mrs. Umney, the housekeeper, was standing on the steps when they arrived. She led them into the library to have tea. Mrs. Otis noticed a dull red stain on the floor. "I'm afraid something has been spilled here," she said to Mrs. Umney.

"Yes," replied the old housekeeper, "that is blood."

"Well, I do not care for blood in the library," said Mrs. Otis. "Please remove it at once."

The old woman smiled. "That is the blood of Lady Eleanor. The bloodstain cannot be removed. And her husband, Sir Simon, still haunts this house."

"That is nonsense!" cried Washington, the oldest Otis son. "Pinkerton's Champion Stain Remover will clean it up in no time."

He scrubbed the spot and the stain was gone.

Just then, a flash of lightning lit up the room. Mrs. Umney fainted. Mr. Otis came into the room and found Mrs. Umney on the floor. He splashed cold water on her face.

"Mr. Otis," Mrs. Umney said, "beware of the ghost that haunts this house."

"Thankfully, we are not afraid of ghosts," said Mr. Otis.

The next morning, Mr. Otis and Washington found the bloodstain in the library again.

"I don't think it is the Champion Stain Remover that is to blame," said Washington. "It must be the ghost." Each morning, they found a fresh stain on the floor. Mr. Otis was beginning to think the ghost existed after all.

One night, Mr. Otis was awakened by a curious noise outside his room. It sounded like the clank of metal. Right in front of him was a ghostly old man.

"Dear sir," said Mr. Otis, holding up a bottle. "Kindly oil your chains with this Rising Sun Lubricator. I must get some sleep."

The Canterville Ghost threw down the bottle and disappeared through the wall. He went to his secret chamber. He was greatly insulted. He thought of all the people he had frightened in the last three centuries. "They never treated me like this," he said. All night he thought about his revenge.

The next night, the ghost appeared again. The family had just gone to bed. Suddenly, they heard a fearful crash in the hall. Mrs. Otis rushed downstairs. There she found a large suit of armor scattered on the floor. The Canterville Ghost sat on the stairs holding his head in his hands.

"Stop! Hold up your hands!" shouted the twin boys. They had brought their slingshots with them. Each of them fired a shot at the poor ghost.

Just then, Mrs. Otis leaned over and offered some medicine to the ghost. "You are far from well," she said. "I have brought you a bottle of Dr. Dobell's Soothing Remedy."

The ghost glared at Mrs. Otis. With a groan, he vanished in the air.

The ghost retreated to his room. He was very upset. "How could they treat me this way?" wondered the ghost. "It's humiliating!"

The ghost felt very ill after this. He hardly left his room, except to put the bloodstain on the floor in the library.

When he recovered, the ghost resolved to try again. He planned to go quietly into Washington's room. Then he would mumble and mock him at the foot of his bed. Then he would go see the twin boys. He planned to sit on them until they screamed. "What a marvelous plan," he thought.

That night, the ghost set out down the hallway. He waited for the clock to strike twelve. A raven croaked from an old tree outside. The wind rattled the shutters on their hinges. "What a perfect night for a scare," thought the ghost.

The ghost chuckled to himself and turned the corner. Suddenly, he wailed and fell back in terror. Right in front of him stood a horrible ghost. Its head was round, fat, and orange. Its eyes were empty black holes. It laughed at him with an awful grin.

The Canterville Ghost had never seen another ghost before. Naturally, he was very frightened. After a second glance at the strange phantom, the Canterville Ghost covered his eyes and ran back to his room. In his bedroom, the ghost hid his face in his blankets.

As the sun came up, the ghost gained some courage. He decided to talk to the other ghost. "Perhaps he can help me scare the twins," thought the ghost.

The ghost tiptoed down the hallway. He reached the spot and gasped. Something had happened to the ghost. It no longer looked frightening. The Canterville ghost could see that the ghost's head was only a pumpkin. He read a sign that said "YE OTIS GHOST."

The Canterville Ghost had been tricked!

YE
OTIS
GHOST

A few days later, Virginia Otis went riding and tore her skirt. She knew her mother would not be happy! Virginia went to the sewing room, hoping to fix her skirt before her mother saw it. When she opened the door, she was surprised to see the Canterville Ghost! He was sitting by the window, watching the leaves fly by. He looked very sad.

Virginia felt sorry for the ghost. "My brothers are leaving tomorrow for school," she said. "If you behave yourself, no one will bother you."

The ghost turned around. "It is my job to misbehave," he said.

"Nonsense!" said Virginia. She turned to leave.

"Please don't go, Miss Virginia," cried the ghost. "I am so lonely, and I don't know what to do. I want to go to sleep, but I cannot."

"That's absurd," said Virginia.

"I have not slept for three hundred years," he said sadly. "And I am so tired. I wish to fall asleep and never wake," said the ghost. He continued to explain why he haunted the old house. The ghost needed Virginia's pure heart. If she would be his true friend, the ghost could sleep forever.

Virginia considered the ghost's request. She stood up and said, "I will help you." She took the ghost's hand and followed him through the wall.

About ten minutes later, the bell rang for tea. Mrs. Otis was greatly alarmed when Virginia did not appear. Mr. Otis rode his horse across the countryside to search for her. He could not find her.

Then at midnight, a panel at the top of the stairs flew open. Virginia came out looking very pale and tired. She was holding a small white box.

"My child!" cried Mr. Otis. "Where have you been?"

"Papa," said Virginia quietly, "I have been with the ghost. He is dead now."

Virginia led them down a secret corridor. Finally they came to a great oak door. Virginia opened it. They found themselves in a small room. A huge iron ring was attached to the wall. A chain led from the ring to a skeleton.

Virginia explained that Sir Simon was locked in this room long ago. "Now he can rest," she said.

Four days later, the Otis family had a proper funeral for Sir Simon. After the funeral, Virginia remembered the white box the ghost had given her. She brought it to her father. Slowly, Mr. Otis opened the box.

Virginia gasped. "Look at those beautiful jewels," she cried.

Virginia's father handed them to her. "You must take them," he said. "We certainly want Sir Simon to rest in peace."

King of Cats

Adapted by Suzanne Lieurance
Illustrated by Kallen Godsey

The grave digger's wife sat by the fireplace. She was mending socks. Her lazy black cat slept on the floor next to her. It was very late. The woman was waiting for her husband, the grave digger, to come home.

The grave digger's wife and the lazy black cat waited and waited. Still, the grave digger did not come home. At last, the grave digger rushed into the house. He slammed the door. His heart was pounding. He was out of breath.

"I have a story to tell you," he said.

He took off his hat and scarf. Then he turned to face his wife.

The grave digger's eyes were wide. He was pale. The grave digger's wife stared at him.

"You look strange," she said. "Did something happen?"

"Yes," said the grave digger. "Something did happen."

The lazy black cat sat up. He stared at the grave digger now, too.

The grave digger's wife moved closer to her husband.

"So tell me," she said. "What happened to you tonight that made you look so pale and afraid?"

The grave digger took a deep breath.

"Well," said the grave digger. "I was digging old Mr. Ford's grave. I guess I fell asleep. I woke up when I heard a cat say, 'MEOW!'"

"Meow!" said the wife's lazy black cat.

The grave digger's eyes widened even more. He pointed to the cat.

"Yes, just like that!" said the grave digger. "I was very deep in the grave. I looked up over the top of it. What do you think I saw?"

The grave digger's wife frowned.

"Now, how would I know that?" she asked.

"Well," said the grave digger. "I saw nine black cats. Nine black cats, just like your lazy black cat here. And what do you think they were doing?"

The grave digger's wife and her lazy black cat looked at each other. Then they looked at the grave digger. The wife shrugged.

"They were carrying a coffin," said the grave digger.

The grave digger's wife gasped.

"A coffin?" she asked.

"A coffin," he said. "There were four black cats on each side of the coffin. One black cat was in front of it. The coffin was covered with a black cloth."

“The cats came closer,” said the grave digger. “They said ‘MEOW!’”

“Meow!” said the wife’s lazy black cat.

“Yes, just like that!” said the grave digger. “As the cats came closer and closer, I could see them more clearly. Their eyes were shining like little lights. They kept coming. They got closer and closer. They were looking at me, just like your cat looks at me now. Why, he looks like he knows every word I am saying.”

“Never mind my cat,” said the wife. “Go on. What happened next?”

“The cats came towards me,” said the grave digger, “very slowly. With every third step they cried out, all together, ‘MEOW!’”

“Meow!” said the wife’s lazy black cat.

“Yes,” said the grave digger, “just like that. When they stood at Mr. Ford’s grave, they all got very still. They looked straight at me.”

Now the grave digger stared back at his wife’s lazy black cat.

“Look at your cat,” said the grave digger. “He’s staring at me.”

“Never mind my cat,” said the wife. “Go on!”

“The one that wasn’t carrying the coffin came even closer,” he said.

The wife’s lazy black cat moved closer to the grave digger. The cat stared straight at him.

The grave digger backed up. He shivered.

"Never mind my cat," said the grave digger's wife.

The lazy black cat's eyes were shining like little lights.

"Go on," she said. "What did the cat do then?"

"The cat moved closer and closer to me," said the grave digger. "Finally, we were nose to nose."

"Oh, my," said the grave digger's wife. "Then what happened?"

"The cat spoke to me!" said the grave digger. "He said, 'Tell Old Tom that Old Tim is dead.'"

The wife's lazy black cat jumped up.

The grave digger's wife screamed.

"Look! Look at my lazy black cat!" she said "What is happening to him?"

The lazy black cat stretched and stretched. He grew taller and taller. Soon he was three times his normal size.

At last, the cat spoke. "What?" he said. "Old Tim is dead? Well, I'm Old Tom. Now I am the King of Cats!"

And with that, Old Tom rushed up the chimney.

The grave digger and his wife never saw the lazy black cat again.

The Mystery on the Sargasso

Written by Lynne Suesse
Illustrated by Jan Gregg-Kelm

John Fields sat on the sand. He looked out over the endless Sargasso Sea. He saw nothing but blue water. He had been stranded on this tiny island for an entire week. He had seen seven sunrises and seven sunsets.

"Good morning, sun!" John would say each morning. At night, he talked to the moon and tried to count the stars.

While he sat on the island, John thought about the storm that had brought him there. He remembered the way his tiny sailboat was tossed about on the waves. He remembered falling into the water. Finally, he remembered waking up in the very spot where he sat now.

John kept busy by fishing for food. He collected coconuts that fell from the trees. The husks of the coconuts were hard to open. But the sweet milk inside was a welcome reward.

Most days, though, John sat and looked at the water. One day, John saw a dot on the water. The dot was a ship! Even though the ship was far away, John could see that it was getting closer. He jumped up and down. He yelled and waved his arms. He would be saved!

As the ship sailed near John's tiny island, he yelled even louder. John ran out into the water. He laughed and waved at the boat.

Soon the ship was near the shore. A crew member rowed a small lifeboat over to John's island.

"I'm happy to see you," John said to the man in the boat. He climbed in. John was so excited, he had trouble sitting still.

The man rowed John back to the ship.

Aboard the ship, the captain and crew welcomed John. "You are a very lucky man," said the captain. He shook John's hand.

"Thank you," John said over and over. He knew that he was very lucky. As he looked around the ship, though, John noticed that things were strange. The captain and crew were wearing unusual uniforms. They were Americans, like John, but he felt that they were very different.

"Welcome aboard *The Lily Belle*," said a crew member, as he led John into a ballroom. "You must be very hungry," said the man. John was very hungry. He was tired of fish and coconuts.

John walked through the ballroom. He saw many people having fun. But, again, something about these people made John feel strange.

The crew member showed John a table covered with food. "Enjoy! Eat as much as you like," he said.

John stood at the table, filling a plate with delicious treats. He could not believe how hungry he was! He did not bother to sit down at one of the tables. He bit into a piece of chicken. He licked his fingers. He looked at all the people in the room.

Suddenly, he realized why these people seemed strange to him. Everyone looked as if they were dressed in a costume! They looked like they were having an old-fashioned costume party. He thought their outfits looked like pictures he had seen from the 1930's. "How fun!" he said to himself.

Soon he was approached by a stranger. She introduced herself as Addie Stewart. "Where did you get that costume?" she asked.

She laughed, but it was a very kind laugh. John thought he must look out of place.

"Your costume is wonderful," said John.

"Costume?" she asked him. "I'm not wearing a costume. This is my favorite dress." Addie stopped smiling.

John realized that he had said something wrong.

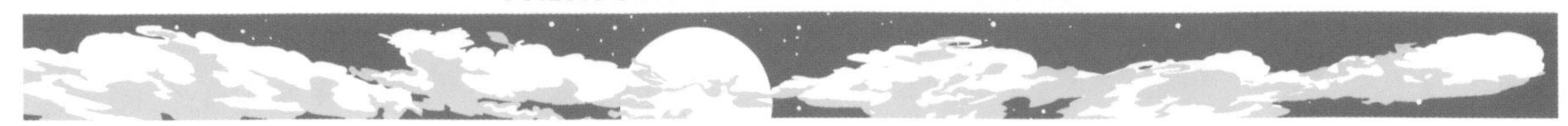

John did not know what to say to Addie. He asked her about the news.

"Have you seen the new bridge?" she asked.

"Which bridge is that?" he asked.

"The Golden Gate Bridge!" she laughed. "It's all anyone talks about."

"Oh, yes. I saw it years ago," said John.

Addie stopped smiling again. "Years ago? Very funny." She thought John was making fun of her.

John felt bad. He did not know what to say. He realized that he was very thirsty, so he excused himself. He went to get a drink.

John got a glass of soda. He looked at a newspaper. The newspaper's date said June 2, 1937! John picked up the paper and read the headline, "Amelia Earhart Ready to Fly Around the World!"

"You guys got props and everything," John said to a man next to him.

"Excuse me?" said the man.

Just then, John heard the bartender's radio. He heard the man on the radio talk about President Franklin Roosevelt. John could not believe his ears! "What day is it? What year?" John asked the stranger.

"Are you serious?" asked the man. "It's 1937."

John ran out onto the ship's deck. "What day is it? I mean, what year is it?" John asked the people on the deck. They laughed. They thought John was just being silly.

John knew that something was wrong. "Can you please tell me who the President of the United States is?" he asked a man and woman.

The couple laughed, but they answered his question. "Roosevelt is the president," said the man. The woman giggled at John.

John knew that he had to leave the ship. Something was very odd on this boat. He felt sick. John looked around and saw the small lifeboats along the side of the ship.

John launched a lifeboat and rowed away. He rowed as fast as he could.

Days later, John was picked up by an American fishing boat. He told the fishermen about the strange ship and the party.

The fishermen looked at each other. John began to describe the ship and the crew. Then John added, "The boat's name was *The Lily Belle.*"

The fishermen were silent. Finally, one of the fishermen said, "The boat you described is a cruise ship. It disappeared in the Bermuda Triangle almost seventy years ago!"

The Bermuda Triangle

Written by Brian Conway
Illustrated by Doug Roy

A long time ago, a new sailboat set sail from Florida. It had twenty-five sailors aboard. The crew was heading south towards the Bermuda islands.

During the voyage, dark clouds began to form over the ocean. One of the sailors used the radio to talk to the crew on a large navy ship.

"Do you have any information about this storm? Repeat: Do you have . . . ," he said. The sailor's message stopped. The radio stopped working.

A young naval officer heard the sailor's message. He tried to use radar to find the sailors to help them. But the sailboat had completely disappeared.

Five years later, the same naval officer was on a search vessel. His radar found a sailboat drifting near Florida.

The young sailor boarded the sailboat. He did not find any people. But it looked like people had recently been on the boat. A warm cup of coffee was on a countertop near the stove. A board game was neatly set up on a table.

When the young officer got back to shore, he looked in the navy's sailing records. He found that this was the boat that had been missing for five years! The records showed that the twenty-five crewmen were never found.

Just southeast of the United States, below Florida, is an area called the Bermuda Triangle. It is in the Atlantic Ocean between Miami, Puerto Rico, and the Bermuda islands. When sailors draw a line from Miami to Puerto Rico, from Puerto Rico to the Bermuda islands, and from the islands back to Miami, what is left on the map is a large triangle.

Many sailors and airplane pilots try to stay far away from the Bermuda Triangle. They report that unusual, unexplained things happen in that area.

Their compasses, the tools that help navigate their direction, spin wildly in the Bermuda Triangle. Clocks and other equipment also display very jumbled numbers. Strange lightning storms are another reason sailors and pilots stay away from that part of the world.

There are also many reports of ships, planes, and all of their passengers just vanishing in the Bermuda Triangle. Some researchers say that over a hundred ships and planes have disappeared. One minute they are there, and the next minute they are gone without a trace.

Even stranger things have happen in the Bermuda Triangle. A missing ship has reappeared, but without any crew aboard. What could cause things like this to happen? What could explain these strange disappearances?

For years, scientists have been trying to figure out what is so different about the Bermuda Triangle. Why do so many odd things happen there?

One answer might be the weather in the area. Hurricanes are common there. It is possible that fast-moving storms surprise sailors and pilots.

But other scientists say the mysteries cannot be explained by bad weather. An accident from a storm would leave some wreckage behind. Usually, rescuers do not find any broken pieces.

Other experts think there might be unusual magnetic energy in the Bermuda Triangle. The magnetic energy draws objects towards it. It makes compasses and clocks break or malfunction. But why does this strange energy cause some vessels to disappear and not others?

Most likely, the pilots and sailors of these crafts are to blame. People who sail for fun sometimes make mistakes or take risks that could cause an accident. Many pilots of small planes are new to flying. It takes a lot of skill to fly a small plane or sail a yacht in bad weather.

But even the most experienced pilots and sailors are afraid of the Bermuda Triangle. They think the dangers of the region can never be explained. Until someone proves that it is safe, they will avoid the Bermuda Triangle.

The Legend of Sleepy Hollow

Based on the original story by Washington Irving
Adapted by Rebecca Grazulis
Illustrated by Jeffrey Ebbeler

There once was a valley that was said to be the quietest place in the world. It was just off the eastern shore of the Hudson River. For as long as anyone could remember, it had been called Sleepy Hollow.

The folks who lived in Sleepy Hollow were a strange lot. They heard voices and saw strange things. It was known that Sleepy Hollow was haunted.

The spirit that most often haunted the enchanted valley was a man riding on his horse. But the man did not have a head. People loved to talk about the ghost.

"He was a soldier," someone would start.

"They buried him in the churchyard," someone else would quickly say.

The people of Sleepy Hollow called this spirit the Headless Horseman.

One of those people was Ichabod Crane, a tall, sweet-tempered teacher. He taught in a plain schoolhouse that stood in a lonely spot at the foot of a green hill. Ichabod's students could not help but think that their teacher's arms and legs were just a bit too long for his body.

"He looks like a scarecrow!" they would whisper as they watched Ichabod walk to school on windy days, his clothes fluttering around him.

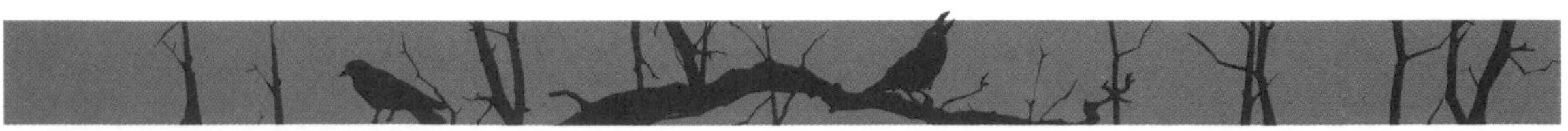

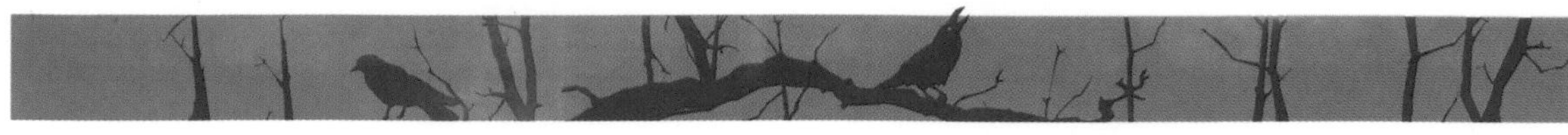

Ichabod loved all scary things, so Sleepy Hollow was the perfect place for him. One of his favorite things to do was stretch out next to the river and read spooky stories.

The only thing that Ichabod loved more than a scary story was a young lady named Katrina Van Tassel. Katrina was one of Ichabod's music students. She was known throughout Sleepy Hollow for her beauty.

"I am only a schoolteacher," Ichabod would say, "but I know I could make her happy."

The only man who Ichabod worried might hurt his chances with Katrina was Brom Bones. With a burly frame and broad shoulders, Brom was a threat to the gangly Ichabod. He was known throughout Sleepy Hollow for his strength and his great skill in horsemanship.

"Oh, Brom Bones!" the women would say. "He is so strong and brave!"

"Wherever there is a fight or a party," the men would chuckle, "Brom isn't far behind!"

Although Katrina showed interest in Brom, Ichabod would not give up.

"I shall not lose!" Ichabod thought. He went about courting the lovely Katrina, visiting her home and taking her for long walks in the moonlight.

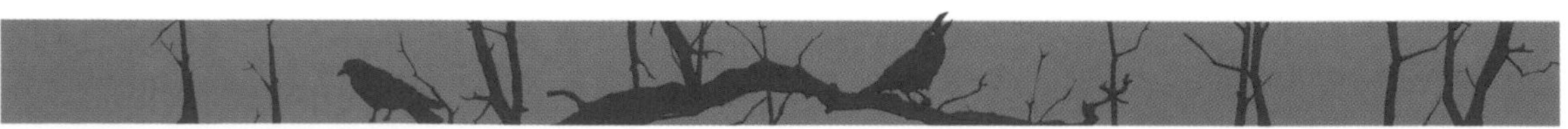

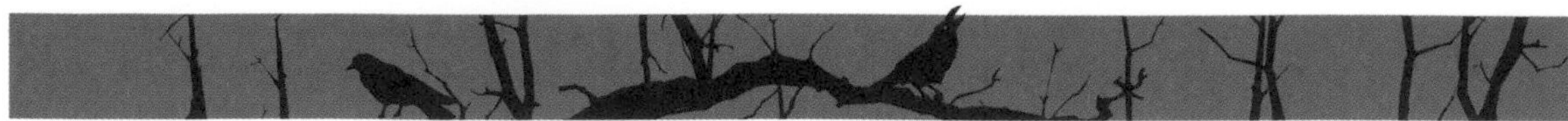

Brom became jealous when he found out that Ichabod was also seeing Katrina. Brom found ways to make things difficult for the young teacher. He began playing practical jokes. One night, he went into the old schoolhouse and turned everything topsy-turvy. Brom always tried to make Ichabod look silly in front of Katrina.

One autumn afternoon, a messenger arrived at Ichabod's schoolhouse to give him an invitation.

"What is the invitation for?" asked his students curiously.

"Why, it is for a party tonight at the Van Tassels'," replied Ichabod. He knew that this was his chance to sweep the fair Katrina off her feet. "She will forget she ever met Brom Bones!" he exclaimed.

The classroom was abuzz with excitement. Ichabod even agreed to dismiss his students a full hour early. He needed time to primp.

After the students burst out of the schoolhouse doors, Ichabod began to groom himself for the big event. He combed his hair, studying his reflection in a mirror that hung in the schoolhouse. Finally, Ichabod stepped back and looked at himself.

"Perfect!" he declared.

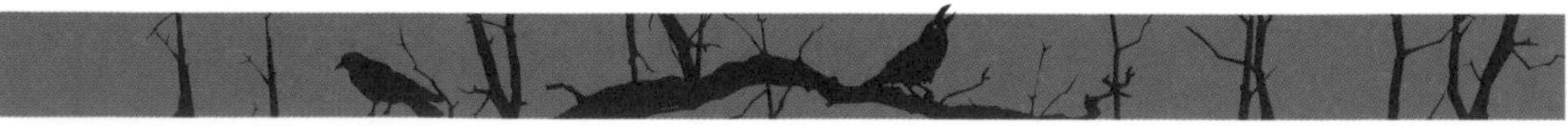

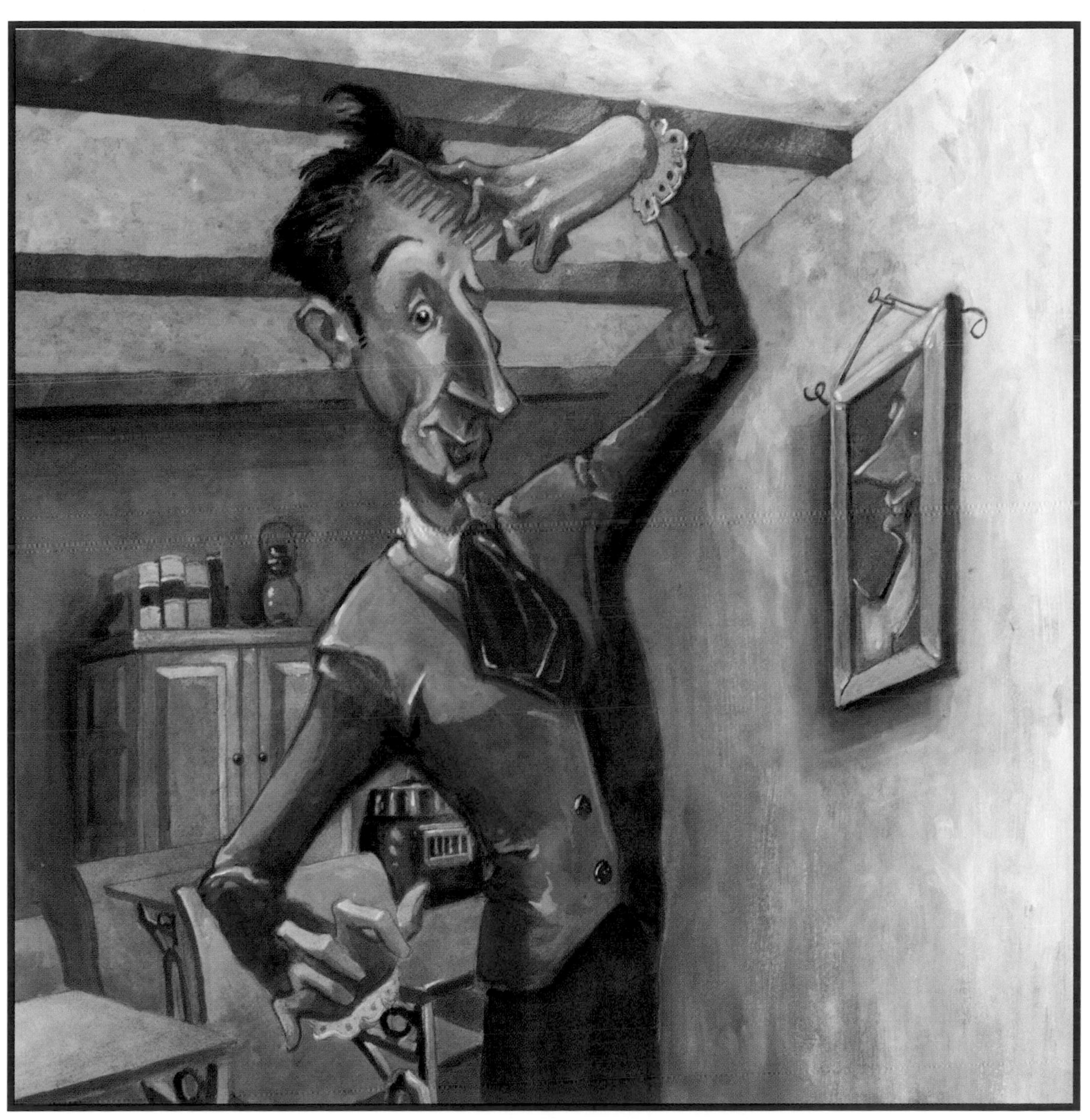

Ichabod proudly mounted his horse like a knight in search of adventure. But he was far from being a brave knight. The horse he rode to the Van Tassels' was not even his own. It was an old plow horse with a tangled mane.

It was a strange sight to see Ichabod riding an old horse. His elbows stuck out like grasshoppers' legs. His arms flapped about like wings. As he rode, his black coat fluttered around him in the wind.

Ichabod was confident when he walked into the party. But his shoulders dropped a bit when he saw his rival, Brom Bones. He was in a corner with some people. Brom had arrived on his favorite horse, Daredevil. Daredevil was just as mischievous as his owner—no one had ever been able to tame him. Ichabod could hear Brom's booming voice.

"And then I lifted all five men with one hand!" Brom bragged.

Ichabod sighed. Would Katrina really choose him over Brom?

Suddenly music floated throughout the manor house and the guests began to trickle into the ballroom.

"May I have the honor of this dance?" Ichabod asked Katrina quickly.

Soon they were whirling across the floor. Katrina smiled happily, but Brom was anything but happy. He stood in the corner, jealously watching Ichabod.

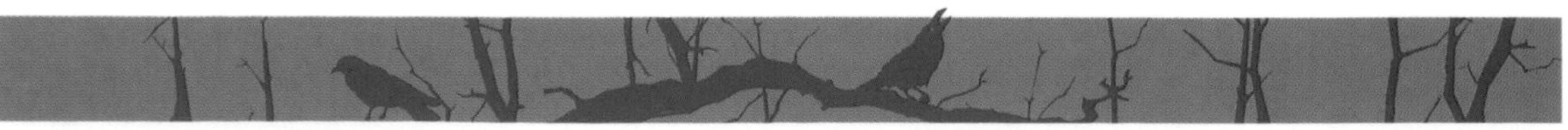

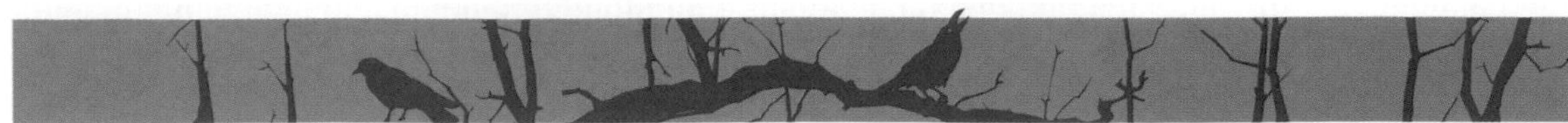

Before Ichabod left the party, he joined a few people who were telling tales of the haunted land. Soon they were talking about the Headless Horseman. It seemed that he had been spotted several times lately.

"He has been seen at one of his favorite places—the bridge that leads to the church," someone said.

It was almost midnight when Ichabod left. There was hardly a sound except for the chirp of the crickets. Even though Ichabod loved all things spooky, he began to feel nervous. His heart was beating loudly. He remembered all of the ghost stories he had heard at the party.

"I must be brave!" said Ichabod, his voice trembling.

Ichabod had never felt so lonely. He began to whistle to keep his spirits up. He thought he heard someone else whistling, but it was just the wind sweeping through the dry autumn branches.

Suddenly, Ichabod jumped in his saddle. Straight up ahead was something white hanging in the middle of a tree.

"A ghost!" yelped Ichabod.

But the nervous schoolteacher saw that it was not a ghost. The tree was only white where it had been struck by lightning.

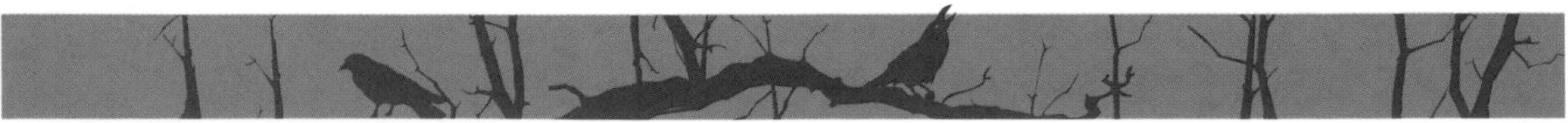

Ichabod was almost at the very spot where the Headless Horseman had been seen. Soon he began to hear a thumping noise. Ichabod turned his head towards the noise. He saw a huge figure standing in the shadows.

"Wh-who are you?" shouted Ichabod.

Ichabod turned his head to get a better look at his unwelcome guest. The figure was a large man riding a great black horse. Ichabod's teeth began to chatter. Then he saw that the man was . . . headless!

"The Headless Horseman!" Ichabod gasped.

"Faster, faster!" Ichabod told his horse.

When Ichabod looked behind him, he screamed in horror. The Headless Horseman was about to throw his head! Ichabod dodged, but it was too late. He fell off his horse. The Headless Horseman rode off into the night.

The next morning, a search party found Ichabod's horse. And a little ways from his horse, they found his hat and a shattered pumpkin.

Ichabod never came back to Sleepy Hollow. When the townspeople told the story, Brom Bones always had a smile on his face. Was it just Brom throwing a pumpkin or did Ichabod really see the Headless Horseman? No one knows for sure. It has become one of the many mysteries of Sleepy Hollow.

White Dog

Written by Renee Deshommes
Illustrated by Brian Floca

Once there was a boy who had a friendly white dog named Ghost. Joey and Ghost were best friends. They loved to roam the countryside looking for adventure. They climbed rocks and waded through cool streams.

Joey's neighbors all liked Ghost, too. One day, Farmer Green saw the two friends walk by his farm. "There goes that boy and his white dog again," he said. "They're lucky to have each other."

That day, Joey and Ghost were hunting squirrels. They never caught any. But the chase was the fun part. Ghost would sniff them out. Then the two friends would run after the squirrel until it hid in a tree.

Suddenly, Ghost spotted a squirrel. Then Joey saw the squirrel. Ghost ran around a rock. When Joey got to the other side of the rock, he stopped. Ghost barked at Joey. "What's wrong, boy?" he asked.

Ghost kept barking until Joey backed up behind the rock. Then Ghost moved. Now Joey could see why his friend was barking. A large black snake was coiled up next to the rock! Ghost had protected Joey.

"What a good boy!" Joey said. "Let's go home."

That night, Joey said good night to Ghost. Then he left a treat for him on the doorstep. "See you in the morning," he said.

The next morning, Joey jumped out of bed and ran downstairs. Outside, he whistled for Ghost. "Gho-o-o-st! Come here, boy," he called. But Ghost did not come. Joey wondered where his best friend could be. He ran to the barn to find his father.

"Have you seen Ghost?" he asked. Joey's dad climbed down from the tractor.

"Son, I found Ghost this morning," his father started. "He wasn't moving, so I took him to Dr. Parker's house. I'm afraid there was nothing he could do. Ghost was very old."

Joey was heartbroken. He would miss his friend so much. He wondered who would explore the woods with him.

After Ghost was gone, Joey spent most of his time alone in the woods. He walked along the creeks where he had once played with Ghost.

One day, Joey ventured farther than he had ever gone before. He was walking along the edge of a ravine. Suddenly, he lost his footing. The rock gave way and Joey landed on a ledge below. Joey's leg was twisted and scraped. He could not climb out of the ravine.

Joey yelled for help. But no one was close enough to hear him.

A few miles down the road, Farmer Green was working in his field. It was a very hot day. He wiped the sweat from his brow. Just then, he noticed a white dog running towards him. It looked like Joey's dog.

The dog barked and barked at Farmer Green. "Hey Ghost, how're you doing?" he said. "Haven't seen you in a while."

The dog continued to bark at him. Farmer Green tried to drive his tractor through the rows of beans. But the dog ran right in front of the tractor's wheels.

Farmer Green blew the tractor's horn. But the dog would not budge. Finally, Farmer Green turned off the engine and climbed down from his tractor.

"Where's your friend?" he asked. "Now go find him."

The dog was very persistent. He continued to bark at Farmer Green. Then he ran up to Farmer Green. He grabbed the man's trousers in his mouth and tried to pull him along.

"Whoa! Okay!" said Farmer Green. "I'm coming. Let's go."

Farmer Green followed the dog through the woods. They wandered for miles through thick brush and tall trees. Every few feet the dog would look back at Farmer Green. He wanted to be sure the man was following him.

They came closer to the ravine. The dog disappeared in the brush.

"Now where did you go?" called the farmer. Then he heard the boy's cries.

Joey was trying to yell for help. He had almost given up. Then he heard a man yelling back to him.

"Hello-o-o!" yelled Farmer Green. "Are you hurt?"

Joey looked up from the ledge. He could see Farmer Green standing at the edge of the ravine. The man was peering down at Joey. He could barely see the boy through the trees.

"I'm okay, but my leg is hurt," Joey yelled back. "I can't make it up there all by myself."

"Hang on," said the farmer. "I'll help you up."

Farmer Green found a strong vine. He held one end of the vine. Then he threw the other end to Joey.

"Use this to pull yourself up," he said.

Joey grabbed onto the vine. It was strong and thick like a rope. Using his good leg, Joey pulled himself up the side of the ravine. Near the top, Farmer Green reached over and pulled Joey onto the rocks.

"Thank you," said Joey. He tried to catch his breath.

Farmer Green helped Joey sit up on the rocks. “Let’s have a look at that leg,” he said. Joey’s leg was still bleeding.

“It hurts,” Joey said, “but I think I can walk.”

“Let’s find a branch you can use as a crutch,” Farmer Green said.

Farmer Green pulled the bark off one end of the branch. Then he helped Joey to his feet.

“You can use this branch as a crutch,” he said. “Now let’s get you home.”

Joey stood up shakily. “Thank you, Farmer Green,” he said.

Joey steadied himself with the crutch. Farmer Green held onto his other arm. Then they hiked through the brush.

When they came to a clearing, Farmer Green spoke. “That’s some dog you got there!” he said.

“What do you mean?” asked Joey.

“I mean, you’d still be sitting in that ravine if that white dog didn’t show me where you were,” said Farmer Green. “He came to my field and barked and barked. Then he led me out into the woods to find you.”

Joey could not believe what Farmer Green was saying. “That couldn’t have been my dog, sir,” whispered the boy. “My dog died almost a month ago.”

A Day At Versailles

Written by Suzanne Lieurance
Illustrated by Jane Chambless Wright

One day in 1901, two women named Anne and Eleanor traveled to France. They wanted to see the palace at Versailles. This palace was Queen Marie Antoinette's home in the late 1700's.

Anne and Eleanor toured the palace. Then they went outside to the gardens. They wanted to find Marie Antoinette's smaller home, a villa.

The women searched for the little villa. Along the way, they saw a deserted farmhouse. They noticed an old plow on the side of the road.

A deep sense of sadness and gloom instantly fell over both women. They felt as if something terrible was about to happen.

Soon the two women discovered they were lost. They did not know where to go until they met two men.

The men were dressed in long green coats. They wore three-cornered hats. The women realized that the men's clothes and hats were odd, too. They were the kinds of clothes soldiers wore during the French Revolution.

"Which way to the villa?" Anne asked the men.

The men pointed down a path. "Follow that path," they said.

It was not long before they found a beautiful gazebo. On a normal day, the gazebo would have been lovely. Yet this did not seem like a normal day. The countryside looked eerie. Anne and Eleanor felt even sadder than before. The trees were still. The birds were silent.

Now the women had stronger feelings of gloom. Something terrible would surely happen soon. But what?

Anne and Eleanor decided to keep going. If they could find the villa, maybe they would feel better.

Suddenly, a man rushed up from behind them. He had a peculiar smile. His face was scarred.

The man stared at Anne and Eleanor. Finally, he said, "You are going the wrong way."

The man pointed to a small bridge. He told the women to go across it. Anne and Eleanor turned and started across the bridge. When they looked back, the strange man was gone.

Anne and Eleanor got to the other side of the bridge. Soon they came to an area they felt must be the villa. Everything was still strangely flat. The countryside looked like something in a bad dream.

Anne noticed a beautiful lady. The lady was sketching the countryside. She wore an old-fashioned dress and a pale yellow scarf around her neck. She looked very sad.

Anne shivered as she looked at this beautiful lady. There was something familiar about her. But who could she be?

Both Anne's and Eleanor's feelings of sadness and gloom grew stronger and stronger. But they could not explain what made them feel so sad.

Anne and Eleanor turned to see a man rush out of a nearby building. He slammed the door. Then he glanced at Anne and Eleanor. "The entrance to the villa is on the other side of the building," he said.

Anne and Eleanor walked around to the other side of the villa. When they got there, they found a small wedding party waiting to tour all the rooms of the villa.

Anne and Eleanor's gloomy mood magically lifted. A soft breeze blew the leaves of the trees.

Anne and Eleanor continued their tour of the villa. Everything seemed normal again. Nothing else unusual happened that day. But the two women did not understand the strange sights they had seen.

The next year, Anne returned to the french palace. She searched for the villa again. But everything looked different.

"Where is the plow?" Anne asked. "The bridge is gone, too."

Anne told a gardener about the men in green coats and the man with the scarred face. Then she described the lady sketching and the man who had rushed out of the villa.

The gardener explained that no plows were kept in the palace gardens. But an old plow had been displayed on the grounds in 1789. No bridge was on the grounds either. But a bridge had been there in 1789. The men in green coats were part of Marie Antoinette's Swiss Guard. The man with the scarred face sounded like an enemy of Marie Antoinette.

The gardener turned to the door that Anne had seen a man rush out of last year. The door was bolted shut.

"It's been bolted shut for many years," said the gardener.

"I know who the lady was," said Anne. "She was Marie Antoinette."

Anne knew she had stumbled into Marie Antoinette's own sad memory. It was her memory of a day in 1789. She had just learned that an angry mob from Paris was marching towards the palace gates to get her.

Yeti

Written by Brian Conway
Illustrated by Jason Wolff

A Sherpa boy named Ang Chiki lived near the mountains of Nepal. His uncle led people on hikes through the icy Himalaya Mountains. Ang was on his first expedition.

Ang slipped and rolled down the snowy mountainside. He was not hurt, but the group was now far ahead of him.

Ang found the group's tracks in the snow. He followed them, hoping to catch up before nightfall.

Ahead of him, Ang saw fresh tracks that crossed the trail. These footprints were large and wide.

Ang put his boot in one. The tracks were deep. They held his feet well. Ang stretched his legs to step in them, one by one.

The footprints led him up the mountain towards the peak. With every long step, Ang was getting closer to the group.

But these huge tracks ended before the peak. They stopped at the opening of an icy cave. It was dark inside.

Ang looked into the cave. It smelled awful!

"Hello!" he called.

From inside the cave, something grunted and growled. Ang stepped back in fright. His face became as pale and cold as the icy cliffs around him. Ang turned around and ran.

The people of Nepal tell stories about wild creatures in the mountains. The Sherpa call them Yeti, which means "snowman." Some people know the Yeti as the "Abominable Snowman."

Some people have seen a Yeti walk standing up, like a person would. Some say they run on four legs like animals do.

They are very fast, even on ice. No one has ever seen a Yeti standing still. Their light-colored hair helps them hide in the snowy mountains.

Many hikers say they have seen these savage snowmen in the mountains of Nepal, Tibet, China, and Russia. They find Yeti tracks in the snow.

One mountain climber took a picture of a footprint in 1951. The track was large. The creature that made it was heavy. It had big toes like a person. It walked through the snow with bare feet.

In 1986, another mountain climber claimed to see a Yeti. He came within thirty feet of the creature.

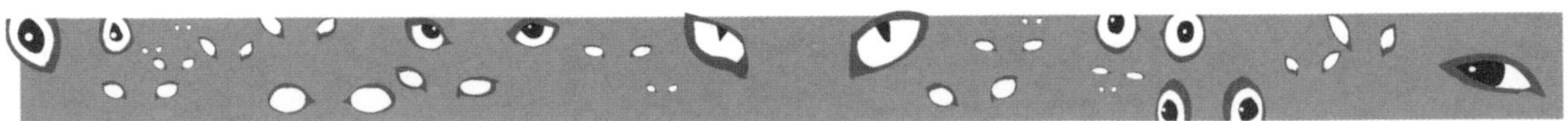

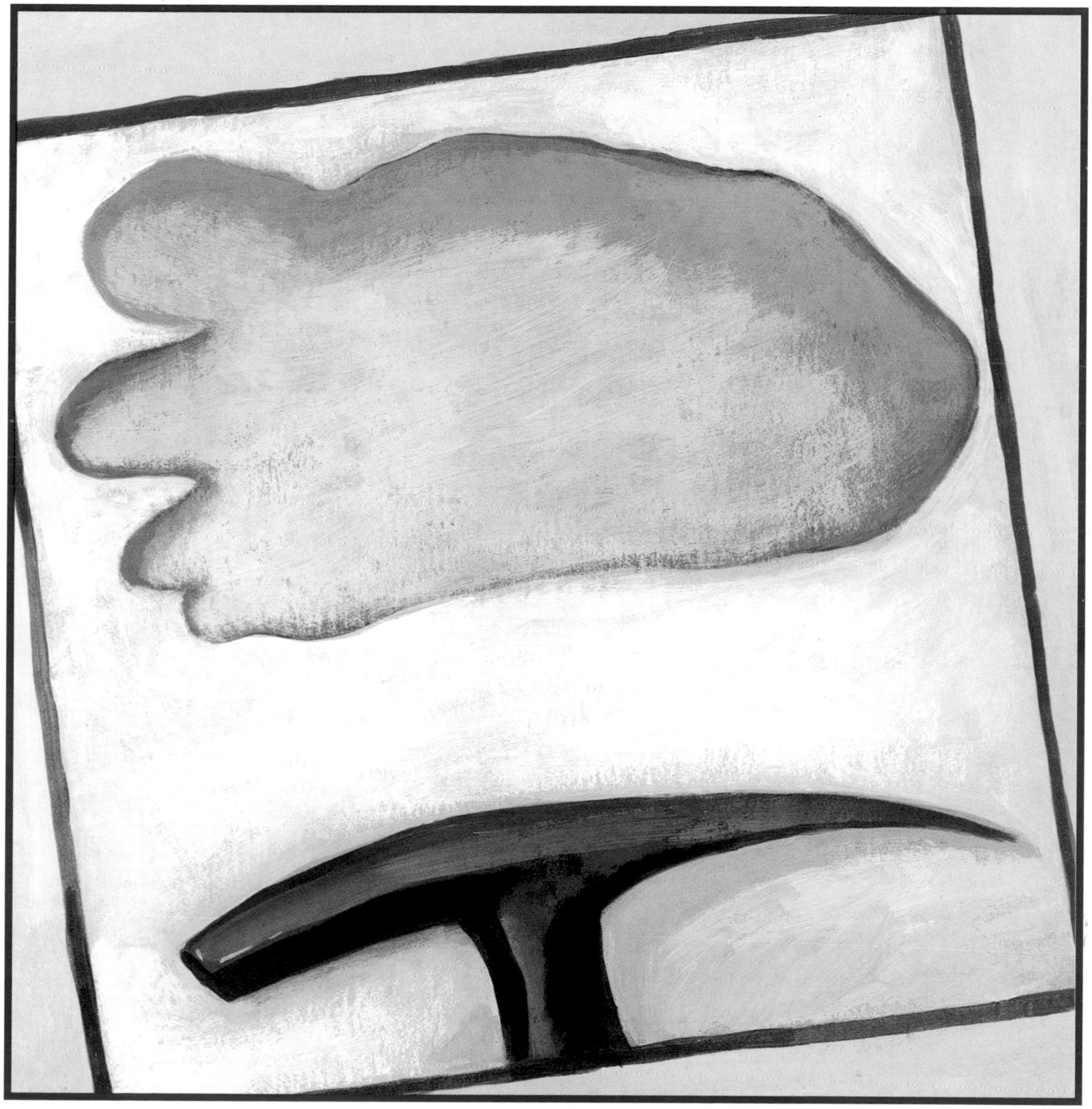

Scientists have searched caves and rocks in the Himalaya Mountains. They found clumps of rough white hairs. They found the bones of a hand trapped in ice for hundreds of years. Was it a prehistoric human hand, or a modern Yeti hand? Tests on the bones did not answer these questions.

A Yeti has never been caught on film. The Sherpa people say the Yeti are too swift. No one will ever catch them, not even with a camera.

One Sherpa guide has said the Yeti are not real. They are only in the scary stories people tell their children.

The Yeti are said to live high in the mountains. Tracks are found in places people rarely go.

Some researchers compare stories of the Yeti with stories about Bigfoot. But Yeti are smaller, and they have white hair. The researchers say the Yeti could be the cold-weather cousin of Bigfoot.

Scientists study about new places all the time. In jungles and oceans where people never go, living species of bugs, birds, plants, and fish are just waiting to be found.

What if scientists studied the rough, icy mountaintops in Nepal? What would they discover?

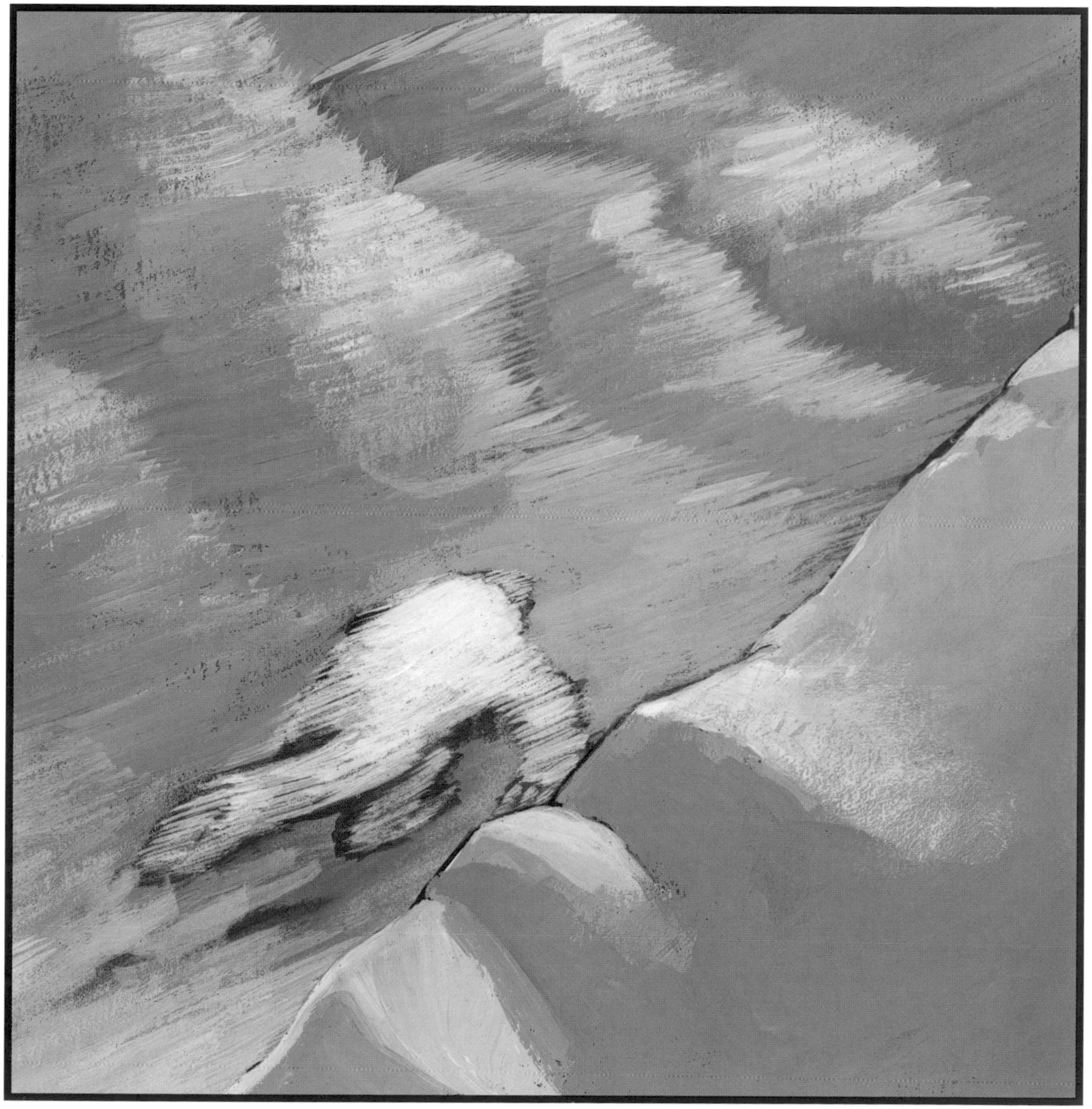

The Monkey's Paw

Based on the original story by W.W. Jacobs
Adapted by Lisa Harkrader
Illustrated by John Kanzler

Mr. White held his front door open. "Morris! Come in, come in." Mr. White's old friend, Sergeant Major Morris, stepped inside. Mr. White led him into the parlor.

Mrs. White and their grown son, Herbert, sat before a crackling fire. Morris settled into a chair. Mrs. White poured tea.

"So good of you to come," said Mrs. White.

"Thank you for inviting me." Morris looked around the parlor. "It's so warm here. So safe. I can almost forget that the mysterious jungles of India lurk right outside this house. I can almost believe life has returned to normal."

"Normal?" Mr. White studied his old friend's face. He looked worried. Or did he look scared?

"Has something happened to you, Morris?" asked Mr. White.

Morris rubbed his hand across his chin. "My life has nearly been destroyed by a monkey's paw."

"A monkey's paw?" Mr. White frowned. "I'm afraid I don't understand what you mean."

Morris reached into his pocket and pulled out a dark object. It was a tiny, shriveled hand, covered in fur.

Mr. White peered down at the tiny hand. "Morris, this is the cause of all your troubles? The withered paw of one small monkey?"

"It's small and withered, yes," said Morris. "But it's powerful. It has a spell on it. This paw grants three wishes to anyone who owns it."

"Three wishes!" Mrs. White looked at the paw. "It's magic then."

"You may call it magic," Morris said. "I call it cursed."

"Cursed?" said Mrs. White. "But that's silly. How can a wish be cursed?"

"Very easily," said Morris, shaking his head. "Whenever we make a wish, greed clouds our judgement."

"I wouldn't let greed cloud my judgement," said Herbert. "I would think the whole thing through. I would know exactly what I was wishing for."

"I thought I was smarter than the monkey's paw and its magic," Morris said. "I was wrong."

"Then you've made your three wishes?" asked Mr. White.

"I have," said Morris. "And if I had a fourth wish, I'd use it now. I'd wish with all my heart I'd never seen this paw. It's terrible, I tell you."

Morris flung the monkey's paw into the fireplace.

"No!" Herbert said. He grabbed a fire iron. Then he fished the monkey's paw from the flames and flipped it onto the parlor floor.

"I can't watch you ruin your happy home." Morris rose to his feet. "You have a fine family and a good life," he told Mr. White. "If you want to keep them safe, you'll toss that cursed paw back into the flames."

Mr. White walked Morris to the door.

When Mr. White returned, Herbert said, "What should we wish for first?"

"Nothing," said his father. "Morris was right. I live in a fine house with a family I love. I have nothing to wish for."

"But this fine house isn't completely ours," said Mrs. White. "We still owe two hundred dollars to the bank. Wouldn't our good life and fine family be that much better without debt hanging over our heads?"

"Think how happy you'd be to hand two hundred dollars to the banker, Papa," said Herbert.

"I don't know," Mr. White said. "It would be nice to own this house." Mr. White stared at the monkey's paw. Then he took a deep breath. "I wish for two hundred dollars."

"Oh!" said Mrs. White. "I saw it move. The monkey's paw moved!"

"It heard your wish, Papa," said Herbert. "Now the wish will come true."

"Nonsense," said his father. "The wind moved it. This monkey's paw is no more magic than I am." He scooped up the paw. Then he put it into his desk drawer. "Let's forget about this withered paw and go to bed."

The next morning, though, Herbert had not forgotten.

"The two hundred dollars may come today while I'm at work," he said, as he left for his job at the factory. "Don't spend it all before I get back."

That evening, Herbert did not come home from work. Mrs. White was very worried. Then a knock sounded at the door. Mrs. White opened the door. A man from Herbert's factory stepped into the hall.

"There's been an accident," the man told Mr. and Mrs. White. "Herbert was caught in the machinery at the factory. We couldn't save him."

Mr. White stared at the man. "Herbert is . . . dead?"

The man nodded. "We hope this will help ease your suffering a bit." He handed Mrs. White an envelope.

Mrs. White's hand trembled as she opened it. "Oh! Oh, no!" She flung the envelope to the floor.

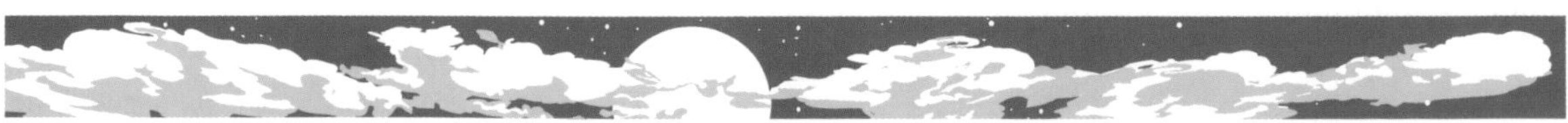

The packet from Herbert's factory contained two hundred dollars.

"Where is the paw?" Mrs. White ran into the parlor.

"I've put it away," Mr. White said, "where it can do no more harm."

"But we have two more wishes," said Mrs. White. "We can wish him back. We can have our sweet Herbert back."

"Do you really think that's wise?" said Mr. White. "After what just happened? Do you believe anything good can come from our wishes?"

"Don't you want your son back?" asked Mrs. White.

"Of course I do," said Mr. White. He unlocked his desk drawer and pulled out the monkey's paw. He closed his eyes. "I wish for my son," he said. "I wish my son Herbert would come back."

Thunder cracked outside the window.

"It heard you," whispered Mrs. White. "Our Herbert will come home."

Mr. and Mrs. White heard footsteps outside.

"Herbert," said Mrs. White. "I'd know the sound of his walk anywhere."

She raced through the hall and flung open the front door.

A tall figure stumbled towards her down the road.

"Herbert!" she said.

Lightning flashed. Mrs. White saw her son clearly.

"No!" Mrs. White screamed. "Oh, no! It can't be." She stared at the figure in the road. It was Herbert, but not Herbert as he had been that morning.

Mrs. White slammed the door.

Mr. and Mrs. White heard Herbert's uneven steps. They heard his knocks on the door.

THUMP. THUMP. THUMP.

"What have we done?" Mrs. White slumped to the floor.

THUMP. THUMP. THUMP.

"We have one wish left," said Mr. White. "I wish…"

THUMP. THUMP. THUMP.

"I wish my son was dead," said Mr. White.

The banging stopped. Mrs. White crept to the window and looked out.

"He's gone," she whispered. "Our son is gone."

"And so are our wishes." Mr. White stared at the shriveled paw in his hands. "Along with our happy life."

He staggered into the parlor and threw the monkey's paw into the fire. And this time Herbert was not there to pull it out.

Sweet Mary

Written by Rebecca Grazulis
Illustrated by Angela Jarecki

Homesville was a nice place—at least that is what the people who lived there said. The people who grew up there liked it so much, they nearly always chose to stay there to raise their own children.

Homesville had all the comforts of a big city, but people always knew their neighbors. When you walked down the street, someone would always smile and ask how you were doing.

Jack was one of Homesville's citizens. Everyone in Homesville knew him and everyone liked him.

Jack had a lot of friends. Jack would spend most of his time playing football, basketball, or baseball with his friends. But he did not have a friend that he could just talk to.

That's when he met Mary.

It happened quite by accident. Jack was sitting in his car in front of the library, daydreaming as usual. He spotted a girl sitting on the bench by the bus stop across the street. She was wearing a party dress and looked like she had been waiting there for quite a long time.

"That's the prettiest girl I've ever seen," Jack said. Jack wanted to introduce himself, but girls always made him nervous. He never seemed to say any of the right things. Finally, he gathered his courage.

Jack reached the bench and sat down. The girl kept staring straight ahead. Jack could feel his heart thumping in his chest.

"Hello," he said shyly.

The girl did not answer.

"My name is Jack," he continued.

Then Jack lightly brushed the girl's shoulder. Suddenly, she came to life. She turned to look at Jack. He could see a touch of fear in her eyes.

"Hello," she said softly, "my name is Mary."

Jack saw that Mary was shivering in the cool autumn air, so he gave her his letter jacket. They sat on the bench for a long time. Jack did all of the talking. Mary just smiled and offered a few kind words.

The hour grew very late. Jack drove Mary home. When Jack stopped in front of her house, Mary leaned over and gave him a quick peck on the cheek. Jack watched Mary walk to the front door. Before Mary went into the house, she turned, looked at Jack, and smiled. It was the sweetest smile Jack had ever seen.

The next morning, Jack picked a small bouquet of flowers and went to Mary's house. A small old woman answered his knock. When Jack asked if he could see Mary, the old woman looked startled.

"Mary?" she asked.

The old woman looked at Jack carefully. Finally, she said, "Please come in."

The old woman pointed to a picture on the mantle.

"Is this the girl you spoke with last night?" she asked.

"Yes," he replied.

"I am Mrs. Sweet—Mary's mother," she said. "Mary died almost twenty years ago."

Jack did not believe what he was hearing.

"Everybody liked Mary," said Mrs. Sweet. "She'd meet someone for the first time and talk to them like she'd known them forever. This house was always full of her friends, laughing 'til all hours," Mrs. Sweet paused. "You're not the first person to tell me that you've seen her. I like to think that she's close."

Jack was shocked.

"It's true, Jack," said Mrs. Sweet. She paused and wiped away a tear. "Mary is buried in the Homesville Cemetery."

Jack left Mary's house and ran until he reached the cemetery. When he saw the letter jacket that he had given Mary hanging on a tombstone, he stopped short. Then he saw what was written on the tombstone:

Mary Sweet

January 14, 1942–May 5, 1958

Jack placed the flowers on Mary's grave. He did not know that Mary's ghost was perched on top of the tombstone, watching him closely.

"I couldn't have imagined you," Jack said. "My jacket is right here!"

Jack reached for his jacket and held it close to him. He noticed that it smelled faintly of perfume.

"You *did* wear this!" he exclaimed. "You *were* at the bus stop!"

Jack began to pace. He was trying so hard to put this puzzle together.

"There were so many things I wanted to talk to you about," Jack said.

Then Mary walked over to Jack and said, "Don't be sad. I'm right here."

Jack could not hear her, but goose bumps rose on his arms at the moment she whispered in his ear.

He did not know that Mary, the sweetest girl he had ever met, had come to say good-bye.

A Ghost Story

Based on the original story by Mark Twain
Adapted by Lisa Harkrader
Illustrated by Ute Simon

I unlocked the door and stepped into my new apartment. I had worked hard all day. I was tired. All I wanted to do was settle in before a cozy fire, read the evening newspaper, then crawl into bed.

I stoked the fire in the fireplace and eased into my favorite chair. In the newspaper I saw a story about the Cardiff Giant:

STONE MAN HAS PLASTER TWIN

Crowds of people have been lining up to see New York City's own "petrified man" at the Eighteenth Street Exhibit Hall. They believe they are paying to see the stone giant that was discovered on a farm in Cardiff, New York. They don't know that the giant on display at the Exhibit Hall is merely a plaster cast of the Cardiff Giant.

Earlier this year, a Cardiff farmer was digging on his farm when he found the stone figure of a man. The stone man was over ten feet tall. Many people believe that an ancient tribe of giants lived in New York thousands of years ago. They believe the farmer in Cardiff discovered the fossilized remains of one of these giant men.

Scientists are now studying the Cardiff Giant. Many experts doubt that the figure is a petrified giant. They believe it is a statue carved from stone.

I laughed. "Some people will believe just about anything. In Cardiff, they were paying to see a stone man that is probably a fake. In New York City, they are flocking to see a plaster imitation of the fake."

At least now, though, I knew why the street outside had been so crowded. I lived across from the Eighteenth Street Exhibit Hall.

I climbed into bed. I was glad I had a scientific mind. I demanded proof when I heard far-fetched stories.

I closed my eyes and was drifting off to sleep when I heard footsteps in the hallway. These were not just any footsteps. They sounded like boulders being dropped on the floor. With each step, the whole building shook. After each step, I heard a *clank*, like somebody was dragging a chain.

THUMP. Clank. THUMP. Clank.

I pulled my blanket over my head. I pressed it against my ears. It muffled the thumping and clanking, but I could still feel the building shake.

The shaking seemed to come closer. My blanket slipped off my shoulders. I tugged on it. Something—or someone—tugged harder.

I pulled the blanket from my face. A huge man loomed over me.

I screamed. The man screamed.

I stared up at the man. His head was the size of my duffel bag; his chest was as big as a barrel. His arms hung down at his sides like tree trunks.

I could see right through him. Through his head I could see the ceiling. Through his enormous belly I could see the fire still crackling in the fireplace.

"You're . . . you're a ghost," I whispered.

"I'm a spirit, it's true," his voice boomed. "A spirit who cannot rest."

His massive shoulders sagged. He looked so sad and lost, I forgot to be afraid of him.

I scrambled from my bed. The poor giant shivered.

"You must be cold," I said. "Come sit by the fire."

He stomped over to the fireplace and heaved his ghostly body into my favorite chair.

Crr-ACK! The chair shattered beneath him.

The giant stood up and looked down at the sticks of wood scattered around him. "I'm sorry. I shouldn't have tried to sit on something so small."

He lumbered over to my bed and lowered himself down on to it.

Crr-INK! The metal bed frame squashed to the floor.

"Stop that!" I said. "You'll crush every piece of furniture I own."

The ghost struggled up from my flattened bed. "I'm sorry. I'm just so tired. I haven't had a chance to sit down for a very long time."

"Here," I said. "Sit on this." I pulled the rug in front of the fire.

"Thank you," he said.

The giant sat on the rug. I wrapped a blanket around his shoulders. I turned my washtub over and set it on his head to keep his ears warm.

"Now," I said, "tell me why you're haunting my apartment."

The ghost sighed. "I didn't want to hurt you. I'm only trying to get some rest. My body is lying across the street. It's on display for crowds of people. I'm so tired. I want to go back to sleep, but I won't be able to until they bury my body again."

"You're the Cardiff Giant!" I said.

"The what?" asked the ghost.

I retrieved the newspaper and spread it open to the story about the giant. "Listen to this," I said.

I began reading the story. I skipped over the part about the scientists who did not believe the stone man was real. I did not want to hurt the ghost's feelings. His eyes grew wide as I read about the plaster imitation.

The ghost stared at me. "The stone man across the street isn't me?"

I shook my head. "He isn't even stone. He's plaster."

The sad ghost buried his face in his hands. "You mean I've been haunting this street for nothing!"

"Don't worry," I said. I reached out to pat his shoulder. "Go to Cardiff. That's where your stone body is."

The ghost rose to his feet. "I'd better get started."

He lumbered across my apartment and walked out the door. His footsteps thundered across the hall and down the stairs.

I glanced at the newspaper. The experts thought the stone man was a fake. I knew he was real. But the experts would never believe me. They would not believe my far-fetched story about talking to a ghost unless I gave them proof.

But I did not have proof. I smiled. I was glad I did not have proof. If the world believed the stone man was a fake, they would leave him alone. Then the giant's spirit would be able to rest.

I heard the ghost stomp out onto the street. I watched the poor ghost of the Cardiff Giant trudge away down the street. Then the ghost turned the corner and disappeared into the darkness.

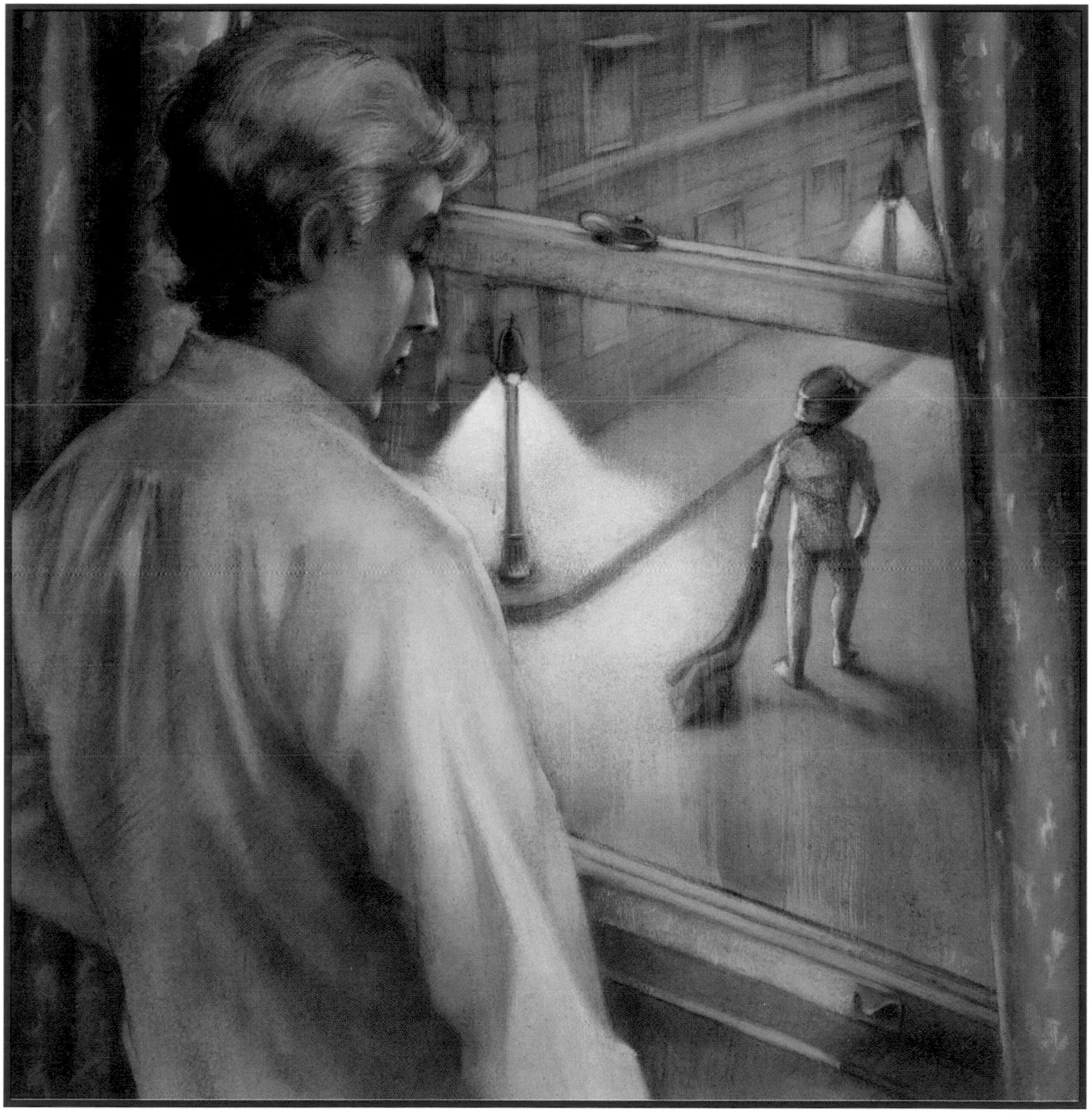

Haunted Cemeteries

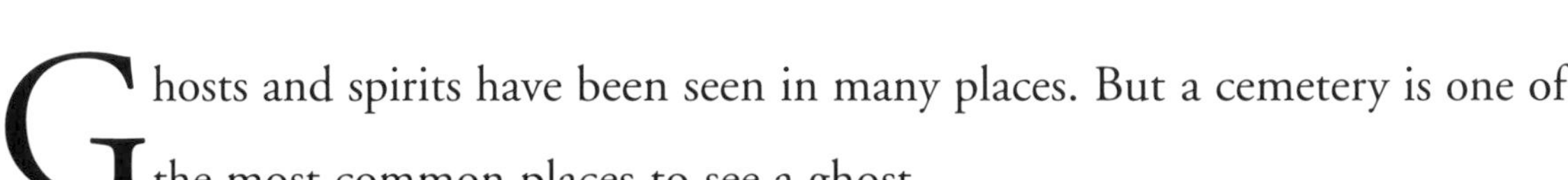

Written by Brian Conway
Illustrated by Jeffrey Ebbeler

Ghosts and spirits have been seen in many places. But a cemetery is one of the most common places to see a ghost.

Bachelor's Grove Cemetery is near Chicago. It is called the "most haunted place" in Illinois.

Over the years, a lot of strange things have happened at Bachelor's Grove Cemetery. Many people have seen the white misty shape of a woman holding a baby. Others have even seen a disappearing house at the cemetery. An eerie light comes from one of the windows, then the whole house disappears.

But the strangest report was about a ghost car. A couple was driving through the cemetery. Suddenly, they saw an old car coming right towards them!

The couple knew they could not swerve out of the way in time. So the man and woman closed their eyes. They expected to crash into the other car. They heard screeching brakes, a loud crash, and broken glass.

But when they opened their eyes, they realized they were not hurt. They looked around. The old car was nowhere to be found. They got out to inspect their own car. It did not have a scratch on it.

Another cemetery where there are almost just as many ghosts as graves is Woodland Cemetery in Dayton, Ohio. One dark night, two college boys were walking home. It was late, so they decided to take a shortcut. They climbed the tall gate to cut through the cemetery.

The boys saw a woman crying on the steps in front of a stone tomb.

"Do you need help?" asked one boy.

As they got closer, the boys noticed they could see right through the weeping woman.

"Are you okay?" asked the other boy.

The ghostly shape looked up at the boys. She had very sad eyes. She stood up quickly and started to float backwards.

She drifted up the steps, passed through the tomb's heavy stone doors, and disappeared. The boys looked at each other.

"Let's get out of here!" they shouted, as they ran away.

When the two students told the cemetery's groundskeeper what they had seen, he nodded. He had heard the story many times before.

"Well," the groundskeeper said, "you're not the first people to meet the Weeping Woman of Woodland."

Ghost sightings at cemeteries usually happen at night. Many ghost experts believe this is when ghosts roam. They say that many spirits cannot find rest in the afterlife. They are cursed to wander all day and night. For this reason, ghosts are sure to be awake when everyone else is asleep.

One famous ghost in Columbus, Ohio, wanders at night. She makes so much noise, she wakes up the neighbors! People who live near Camp Chase Cemetery wake up to hear loud cries in the middle of the night.

The sad ghost is known as the Lady in Gray. Neighbors who have seen her say she is dressed in a gray suit from the 1860's. They say the Lady in Gray is full of sorrow because her husband died in the Civil War. Some believe she is the wife of Benjamin Allen, a soldier who died at Camp Chase during the Civil War. His tombstone is still there today.

Many people have seen the Lady in Gray. One neighbor heard her cry out, "I miss you! Benjamin! Oh, no."

The neighbor thought the cries were a loud prank. He went to the cemetery to investigate. But he did not see the Lady in Gray or anyone else for that matter. But there were footprints in the snow. Then he found two red roses left in front of Benjamin Allen's tombstone.

The Mummy

Written by Renee Deshommes
Illustrated by Patrick Browne

Judsen was a famous archaeologist. She had been exploring tombs with her father since she was a little girl. Now she would take her son, Davis, on his first dig far away in Egypt.

Judsen had received a map from her friend Rashidi. The map showed Judsen where to find King Elysian's tomb. Judsen and Davis would meet Rashidi in Egypt and travel to the tomb together.

"King Elysian was a boy king," Judsen told Davis. "He was ten years old."

"That's how old I am!" said Davis excitedly.

"King Elysian became ill soon after he began his reign," Judsen explained. "He died just before he turned eleven."

Davis listened intently to his mother's story. "The people buried King Elysian in a secret tomb," she explained. "They also buried maps in the tomb. These maps may help us find other secret kingdoms and hidden jewels."

Soon the airplane was flying high above the clouds. Judsen remembered something she did not tell Davis. Rashidi had translated a secret message on the map. It read, "Those who disturb this tomb will be cursed forever."

Finally, the plane touched down in Egypt. Rashidi was waiting at the airport. "Welcome to Egypt," he said. "Are you ready to find King Elysian's tomb?"

As they grabbed their bags, a man approached Judsen.

"Are you the one looking for King Elysian's tomb?" he asked.

"Yes, but how did you know?" answered Judsen.

"Everyone is talking," he replied. "You must not disturb the tomb. The only person to find the tomb disappeared the next day. No one saw him again."

The man left and disappeared into the crowd. "Is that true?" asked Davis.

"I don't believe it," Judsen said. "King Elysian has been dead for thousands of years. How can a mummy put a curse on us?"

Rashidi led Judsen and Davis out of the airport. Soon they were heading for the desert. Three camels were waiting for them. They climbed onto the camels' backs and rode across the desert.

Rashidi and Judsen looked at the map many times. They made many twists and turns. Davis did not know which way they were heading.

Soon they came upon an opening to a cave. "This is it!" shouted Judsen. The three explorers jumped off their camels and ran to the opening. Judsen pointed her flashlight into the hole.

Judsen led the way and climbed down into the cave. They were amazed by all the maps and ancient drawings carved into the walls.

"Mom, what does that say?" asked Davis.

"Those are hieroglyphics," said Judsen. She copied all the pictures in her notebook. "I'm not sure what they say. Rashidi can translate them."

Judsen stopped and studied each picture. She recognized the pictures from the map. They made her feel a little uneasy.

"Davis," she said, "please do not disturb anything." Judsen was backing up to shine her flashlight on the wall. Suddenly she heard a loud crash.

"Oh, no!" said Judsen. She looked down and found an ancient urn filled with jewels. The jewels had scattered across the ground.

"You must leave everything just as you found it," warned Rashidi.

Judsen and Davis scrambled to pick up the jewels. They carefully put the jewels back in the urn. Judsen felt around on the ground for any loose gems. It was very dark in the cave. Judsen did not see that a diamond had rolled into the corner.

"I think we found them all," said Davis.

"Good," said Judsen. "Now let's find that mummy."

Judsen pointed her flashlight down a long corridor. Every few feet, Judsen would stop and copy the pictures into her notebook. Davis began to think the hallway would never end. But soon it emptied into a round room.

"There it is," whispered Davis. Judsen's flashlight stopped on a very small mummy. Davis stood next to the mummy. He ran his hand over the top and then touched his head.

"We're the same size," said Davis.

Judsen noticed the hieroglyphics etched into the rock right behind the small mummy. One showed a young king taking a drink. Another showed the king falling down. Judsen copied these pictures into her notebook, too.

Soon Judsen was finished drawing. "It's time to go," she said.

This time, Rashidi led the way with his lantern. At the opening, Judsen stopped and looked up. She saw hieroglyphics above the opening of the cave.

"I didn't see these earlier," she said. "Rashidi, what do these pictures mean?"

Rashidi held his lantern near the pictures and shook his head. "They are a warning to all visitors," he said. "If anything is disturbed, a curse will follow."

Judsen thought about the jewels in the urn. Then she helped Davis climb out of the cave.

The sun was setting in the sky. “We will ride back to my village. You can stay there tonight,” Rashidi said.

The three explorers climbed back onto their camels and set out across the desert. It was a long ride. Davis could not keep his eyes open. He leaned onto the camel’s neck and fell asleep.

“We are here,” said Rashidi. It was a small home made of stone. Rashidi tied their camels up to a tree. Judsen helped Davis get down. She carried him inside and put him in bed.

Then Judsen and Rashidi studied Judsen’s notes from the tomb.

“These pictures show the king,” said Rashidi, “and how he died.”

“It looks liked he drank something that made him sick,” said Judsen.

Just then, they heard Davis cry out. Judsen rushed into his room. She felt Davis’s forehead. It was very hot.

“Rashidi,” she called, “please find a doctor.” Rashidi ran out in the darkness. Soon he returned with another man. The doctor examined Davis, but he could find nothing wrong with the boy.

“This is the curse of King Elysian,” he said. “You have disturbed his tomb, and he is angry.”

Judsen remembered the jewels she knocked over. "Maybe I didn't pick them all up," she thought. Then she remembered all the pictures she copied into her notebook. "I must return to the tomb," she whispered.

By daybreak, Judsen was back at the cave. She climbed into the opening and read the hieroglyphics above her head. The same pictures were still there. Judsen searched the ground for missing jewels.

Suddenly, she noticed something twinkling in a corner of the cavern. There was a sparkling diamond! Judsen quickly returned it to the urn. Then she carried her notes and sketches down the long corridor.

In King Elysian's tomb, Judsen left the papers at the foot of the mummy. She shone her flashlight on the mummy's face. Judsen took one final look at the boy king.

"You may be small, but you are very powerful," she said.

She followed the corridor to the cave's opening. When she looked up at the hieroglyphics, they were gone! The king's warning had vanished.

Judsen rode back to Rashidi's village. She was relieved, but not surprised, to see that Davis was healthy again.

"I'm ready to go on another adventure!" Davis said.

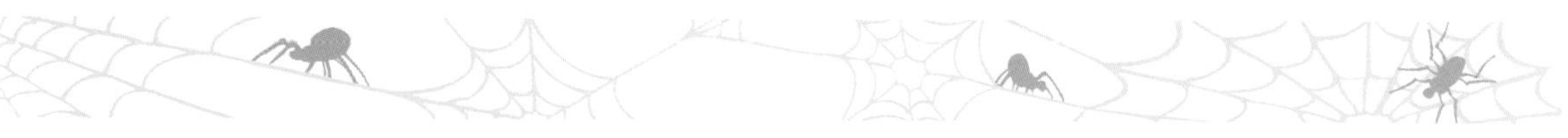

The Teeny-Tiny Woman

Adapted by Suzanne Lieurance
Illustrated by Cathy Johnson

Once upon a time there was a teeny-tiny woman. She lived all alone in a teeny-tiny house. Her teeny-tiny house sat on the teeny-tiny edge of a big swamp. The teeny-tiny woman loved her teeny-tiny house.

One day, the teeny-tiny woman decided to go for a teeny-tiny walk. She put on her teeny-tiny scarf and her teeny-tiny shawl.

She went only a teeny-tiny way before she stopped at a teeny-tiny gate. The teeny-tiny woman walked into a teeny-tiny churchyard.

Inside the teeny-tiny churchyard, she found a teeny-tiny graveyard. The teeny-tiny graveyard had only one teeny-tiny grave. The teeny-tiny woman looked at this teeny-tiny grave. On top of it was a teeny-tiny bone.

"This teeny-tiny bone will make me some teeny-tiny soup. I'll have that for my teeny-tiny supper," said the teeny-tiny woman. She put the teeny-tiny bone into her teeny-tiny pocket.

She left the teeny-tiny graveyard. She opened the teeny-tiny gate to the teeny-tiny churchyard. She walked a teeny-tiny way to her teeny-tiny house on the teeny-tiny edge of the big swamp.

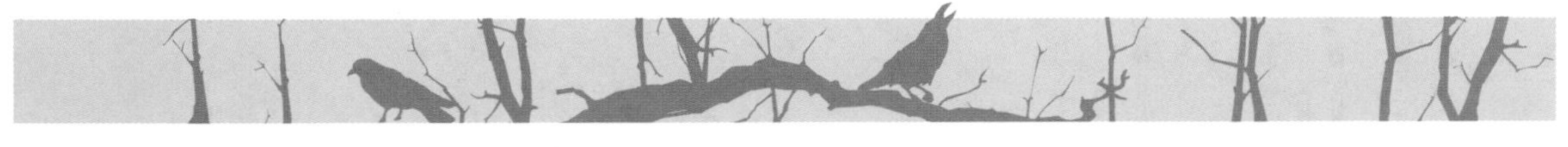

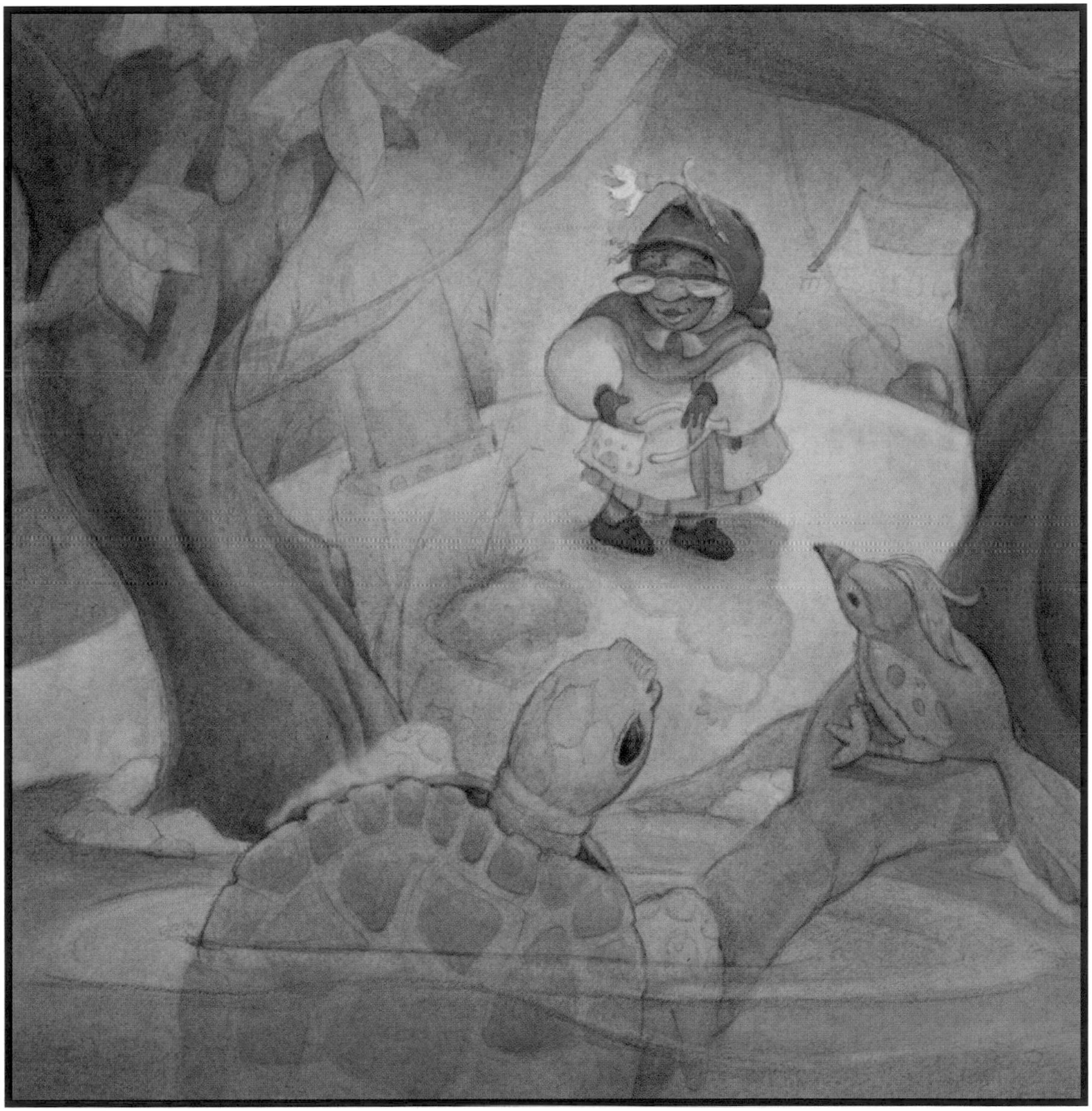

Now the teeny-tiny woman was a teeny-tiny bit tired. She did not feel like making any teeny-tiny soup with the teeny-tiny bone.

The teeny-tiny woman put the teeny-tiny bone into a teeny-tiny jar. She put the teeny-tiny jar into her teeny-tiny cupboard.

"I think I will go take a teeny-tiny nap," said the teeny-tiny woman. She went to her teeny-tiny bedroom. Then the teeny-tiny woman crawled into her teeny-tiny bed. Soon the teeny-tiny woman was fast asleep.

The teeny-tiny woman slept for just a teeny-tiny time. A teeny-tiny voice woke her. The teeny-tiny voice called out from the teeny-tiny cupboard.

The teeny-tiny voice said, "Give me my bone!"

The teeny-tiny woman was a teeny-tiny bit scared. She pulled the teeny-tiny covers up around her teeny-tiny eyeballs.

The teeny-tiny voice in the teeny-tiny cupboard stopped.

The teeny-tiny woman went back to sleep. But only for a teeny-tiny time.

The teeny-tiny voice cried out from the teeny-tiny cupboard again.

It woke the teeny-tiny woman.

This time, the voice was a teeny-tiny bit louder.

"Give me my bone!" it said.

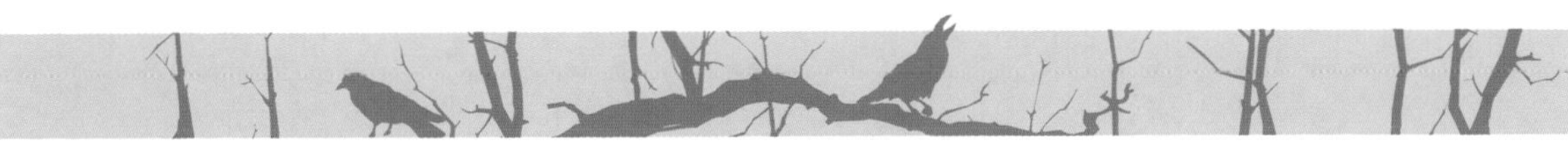

Now the teeny-tiny woman was a teeny-tiny bit more scared. She pulled the teeny-tiny covers over her teeny-tiny head and tried to hide. Soon, the teeny-tiny woman went back to sleep. But only for a teeny-tiny time.

The teeny-tiny voice called out again from the teeny-tiny cupboard. It woke up the teeny-tiny woman. This time, the teeny-tiny voice was just a teeny-tiny bit louder.

The teeny-tiny voice said, "Give me my bone!"

The teeny-tiny woman was a teeny-tiny bit more scared than before. But she did not hide under her teeny-tiny covers.

The teeny-tiny woman poked her head out from under the teeny-tiny covers. In her loudest, teeny-tiny voice, she said, "TAKE IT!"

Then the teeny-tiny woman went back to sleep. The teeny-tiny voice did not call out from the teeny-tiny cupboard anymore.

The teeny-tiny woman slept soundly all night in her teeny-tiny bed. The next morning, the teeny-tiny woman looked in her teeny-tiny cupboard. The teeny-tiny jar and the teeny-tiny bone were gone.

Now the teeny-tiny woman was a teeny-tiny bit hungry again. After all, she never made her teeny-tiny soup for her teeny-tiny supper.

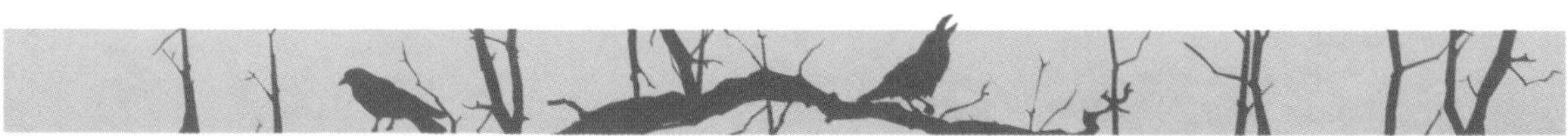

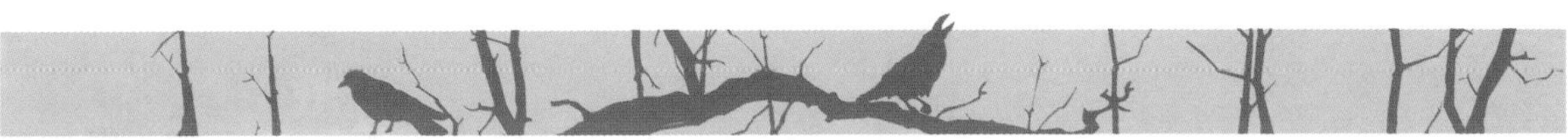

The teeny-tiny woman went for another teeny-tiny walk. The teeny-tiny woman went only a teeny-tiny way.

She stopped at the teeny-tiny churchyard. Inside the teeny-tiny churchyard she found the teeny-tiny graveyard again.

The teeny-tiny woman saw her teeny-tiny jar sat on top of the teeny-tiny marker of the teeny-tiny grave. The teeny-tiny woman picked up her teeny-tiny jar. The teeny-tiny jar was empty.

The teeny-tiny woman was just about to go back to her teeny-tiny house. She noticed something else.

"What is this?" said the teeny-tiny woman. "A teeny-tiny tooth." She put the teeny-tiny tooth in her teeny-tiny jar. She took the teeny-tiny jar back to her teeny-tiny house. She put the teeny-tiny jar into her teeny-tiny cupboard.

Now the teeny-tiny woman was a teeny-tiny bit tired again. She decided to take a teeny-tiny nap. The teeny-tiny woman was almost asleep when she heard a teeny-tiny voice.

"Give me my tooth!" said the teeny-tiny voice.

This time, the teeny-tiny woman knew just what to do.

In her loudest, teeny-tiny voice, she said, "TAKE IT!"

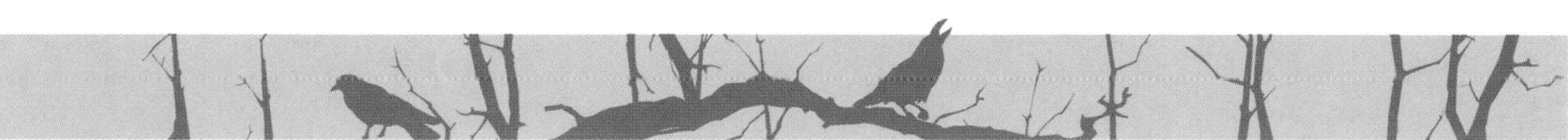

The Open Window

Based on the original story by Saki
Adapted by Elizabeth Olson
Illustrated by Jenifer Schneider

Vera smiles at Mr. Nuttel. "My aunt will join us soon," says Vera. "Until then, you must try and put up with me. May I take your hat and coat?"

Mr. Nuttel is a nervous man. He shyly smiles back at Vera. "Thank you," he says. He gives her his hat and coat.

Mr. Nuttel nervously looks around the drawing room. He looks at all the pictures on the walls and the couch. He looks at the open window. He looks at the green lawn just beyond the open window.

Vera closely watches Mr. Nuttel.

"You just moved to the country?" she asks.

"Yes," says Mr. Nuttel. He fidgets with his hands. His eye twitches. "I moved here to benefit from country life. Country life is relaxing and slow."

"Do you know anyone in the country?" asks Vera.

"Not a soul," says Mr. Nuttel. "Your aunt, Mrs. Sappleton, is my first new friend." Mr. Nuttel takes a deep breath. His body shivers. "My sister, Olivia, lived in the country four years ago. Olivia met your aunt at that time. Olivia says your aunt is very nice."

"So you don't know anything about my aunt?" asks Vera.

"I only know her name and address," says Mr. Nuttel. "Is she nice?" he asks with a gulp.

"Oh, yes, very nice indeed," says Vera. "She is nice despite the tragedy."

"Tragedy? What do you mean?" asks Mr. Nuttel. He fidgets with his hands. His eye twitches. His body shivers.

"The tragedy happened about three years ago, since your sister was here," says Vera. Vera looks directly into Mr. Nuttel's eyes. "You may wonder why this window is open," she says.

"I had noticed it," says Mr. Nuttel. "The view is very pretty."

"Pretty and tragic," says Vera. "Three years ago today, my aunt's husband, two brothers, and their favorite dog left through that window on a hunting trip. They never returned. They had gone hunting on the moors. When they crossed a moor, they fell into a deep bog and were never seen again."

Mr. Nuttel's eyes widen with fear.

"On the anniversary of their deaths," says Vera, "my poor aunt leaves the window open. She believes that they will return. And, you know, Mr. Nuttel, on such a lovely day as this, I sometimes think they will."

Vera's aunt walks into the room. "Mr. Nuttel," she says, "I am sorry to keep you waiting. I hope my niece has made you comfortable."

"Y-y-y-es," says Mr. Nuttel, his eyes looking quickly from Mrs. Sappleton to Vera to the window.

"I do hope you don't mind the open window," says Mrs. Sappleton. "My husband and brothers are hunting on the moors. They should return soon. They always come back through this door. I do hate how they track mud onto my carpets. Those moors are so muddy, you know."

Mr. Nuttel listens with horror. He fidgets with his hands. His eye twitches. His body shivers. Vera watches Mr. Nuttel.

"I-I-I see," says Mr. Nuttel, anxious to change the subject. "I am pleased to meet you. I will be in the country for a few months. I moved to the country for the benefit of my nerves. My doctor says I absolutely must relax. Country life is relaxing and slow, don't you think?"

Mrs. Sappleton turns from the open window. She looks at her guest. "Yes, it is, Mr. Nuttel," she answers. "And the hunting in the country is very good, too."

Mrs. Sappleton turns back to the open window. "I wonder how the hunting is today?" she asks.

The drawing room is silent.

Mr. Nuttel nervously tries to fill the silence. "My sister, Olivia, met you about four years ago," he says. "Olivia said the country would be very good for my nerves."

"Look! Here they are," says Mrs. Sappleton. "And they're back just in time for tea." The older woman walks towards the open window. She looks out across the green lawn. "Goodness! Look at all that mud. They will surely ruin all of my carpets today."

Mr. Nuttel cannot believe his eyes and ears. What a tragic situation. This poor Mrs. Sappleton needs more help than he does. Mr. Nuttel turns to Vera to show his sympathy, but the child is staring out the window. Vera's eyes are wide with horror.

Mr. Nuttel fidgets with his hands. His eye twitches. His body shivers. He turns to look out the window.

Far across the green lawn, a dog runs toward the drawing room. Following the dog is an older man with a shotgun resting on his shoulder and two young boys carrying sacks. Their boots are covered in mud.

Mr. Nuttel screams, "AAARRRGGGHHH!"

Mr. Nuttel grabs his coat and hat. Without turning back, he runs from the drawing room and out the open window. He runs across the lawn and disappears from sight. In his hasty exit, he almost knocks over the returning Mr. Sappleton.

"What got into that young man?" asks Mr. Sappleton. He steps on the clean carpet with his muddy boots.

Mrs. Sappleton shakes her head and looks at the mud.

"Such an odd, nervous fellow," Mrs. Sappleton tells Mr. Sappleton. "He fidgeted with his hands. His eye twitched. His body shivered. He talked all about his nervous condition. Then he left without saying good-bye. Very peculiar."

"He was probably frightened by the dog," says Vera. She bends to scratch the dog's head.

"Makes sense, really," Vera continues. "He told me that he was very scared of dogs. Several years ago he was hiking in the mountains. While following a dark and narrow trail, he stumbled upon a pack of wild dogs. The dogs chased the poor fellow for three days. Mr. Nuttel finally climbed up a tree and hid in the branches. Below him, the dogs walked back and forth, snarling and barking, for a whole week."

Vera sweetly smiles at her aunt and uncle. Vera likes to tell stories.

Dracula's Secret

Based on the original story by Bram Stoker
Adapted by Elizabeth Olson
Illustrated by Jeremy Tugeau

Galloping horses pull a coach along a dark road. The driver shouts to his passenger. "We will arrive at the castle soon," he says. "I'll drop you off and leave at once. I must get out of these woods before the moon rises. Strange things happen around here during the full moon."

"What kind of things?" asks Jonathan Harker.

"When the moon is full," says the driver, "wolves prowl about and bats fly the skies. The wolves and bats travel with vampires."

"There's no such things as vampires," says Jonathan.

Jonathan sits back in the coach. He is too tired to be scared. He has been traveling for weeks.

Jonathan carries a packet with a secret document from London. His boss, Mr. Hawkins, asked him to give the document to Count Dracula of Transylvania.

"Whoa!" shouts the driver. The coach stops. Jonathan steps out. In front of him is a dark castle with an iron door and several towers. "Here's your stop, the castle of Count Dracula."

Before Jonathan can thank the driver, the coach speeds away.

Jonathan pulls the rope next to the door. The bell rings—*ding-dong.* A man in an elegant suit stands in a dark hallway.

"Welcome to Transylvania, Mr. Harker," he says. "I've been expecting you." Count Dracula steps forward and shakes Jonathan's hand. The strength of the grip scares Jonathan. A chill travels up his spine.

"Thank you, Count Dracula," says Jonathan. The count's skin is as pale as the full moon, which rises in the sky. Jonathan hears a wolf howl in the distance. Bats flap overhead.

"Listen to the welcoming sounds of the night," says the count.

Jonathan shudders. "You have an interesting country," he says.

"You must be very hungry after your long journey," says the count. "Come. Dinner is ready."

Jonathan follows the count to the dining hall. Heaping plates of food are on the table. He forgets his fear and sits down. From his place at the table, the count watches Jonathan. The count's plate is empty. He does not eat.

"Count Dracula," says Jonathan. "Won't you join me?"

"I will eat later," says the count. The count smiles. Two sharp, white teeth glimmer in the candlelight.

After dinner, the count shows Jonathan to his room. “Sleep as long as you like,” says the count. “I won’t be home tomorrow until after dark.”

“Thank you for your hospitality,” says Jonathan. “Before you leave, I have something for you.” Jonathan gives the packet to Count Dracula. “This packet contains a secret document from my boss, Mr. Hawkins.”

Dracula smiles widely. He takes the packet. “Ah, yes,” he says. “I have been waiting a long time for this.”

That night Jonathan does not sleep well. Howling wolves and flying bats haunt his dreams.

The next day, Jonathan explores the castle. He tries to open the other doors along the hallway. They are all locked.

Finally, he tries a heavy door at the top of the stairs. The rusty latch breaks in his hand. The door swings open to reveal a stairway. He follows the twisting stairs deep beneath the castle.

At the bottom, he enters a dark, earthen room lit by torches. Several wooden boxes rest on the floor.

Puzzled, Jonathan kneels near one of them. He slowly pulls back the lid. He almost screams. The box contains Count Dracula. He is a vampire.

Jonathan runs from the room. He races up the staircase. Back in his room, he quickly packs his bag. "I must leave this place at once," says Jonathan. Through his window, Jonathan sees the sun is low in the sky. "Night will be here soon. I must have slept for most of the day."

Jonathan runs to the iron door at the castle entrance. Three wooden beams cross the door. "The count has locked me inside the castle!" shouts Jonathan. "I am a prisoner. But I am smarter than he thinks. I will escape."

Jonathan looks around the dark hallway. He sees the count's lamp on a table. By the light of the flickering flame, Jonathan searches the walls.

At last he finds a bin below a small door in the corner. "This must be for the coal deliveries," says Jonathan. He turns the door's tiny knob. The door swings open. Quickly, Jonathan squeezes through the door. He falls to the ground on the other side.

Just then a wolf howls in the distance. Bats fly from the castle towers. The sun begins to sink below the trees. "I must leave at once. This is a very strange land. Vampires sleep by day and walk at night."

Jonathan sees a horse near the castle walls. He jumps on the horse's back. The frightened animal gallops from the castle, carrying Jonathan to safety.

After many weeks, Jonathan arrives back in London. His wife, Mina, is happy to have him home. "I'm so happy you are with me once again. Strange things are happening in London. I do not want to be alone," she says.

"What has happened?" asks Jonathan.

"Bats have been flying over the city," says Mina. "I hear wolves howling."

"Bats and wolves in London?" asks Jonathan. "That's silly. Bats and wolves live in Transylvania, not London. There must be some logical explanation. My poor Mina, why don't we go to the theater tonight? That will take your mind off such strange things."

"Maybe you are right," says Mina.

Jonathan and Mina dress in evening clothes. They attend a play. Then they stroll along the city sidewalks.

"What a fine play," says Jonathan. "What a lovely night, too."

"You were right," says Mina. "I do feel better. Look at the full moon. Isn't it just beautiful?"

Just then a man in an elegant suit passes them on the sidewalk.

"Good evening, Mr. Harker," he says. Jonathan turns to face him. The man smiles. Jonathan sees two sharp, white teeth. The man is Count Dracula.

Jonathan cannot believe his eyes. The count is in London. "Mina," says Jonathan, "I must visit my boss, Mr. Hawkins. I have an urgent question to ask him. But, first, I will take you home."

"You are acting strangely," says Mina. "I hope everything is okay."

Jonathan walks Mina home. He then runs to Mr. Hawkins's house. As he knocks on the door, Jonathan hears a wolf howl. Bats fly across the night sky. Jonathan shudders.

"Hello, Jonathan," says Mr. Hawkins. "It's a pleasure to see you."

"I'm sorry for the lateness of the hour, sir," says Jonathan. "I must know the meaning of the document I gave Count Dracula."

"Is that all? Count Dracula had requested that the document remain secret," says Mr. Hawkins. "But I can tell you now. The document you gave him shows that he owns a house in London. With that document, he can move here."

"H-h-he can move here? Count Dracula is going to live in London now?" shouts Jonathan.

Mr. Hawkins smiles.

"You're going to have a new neighbor," says Mr. Hawkins. "Count Dracula bought the house right next to yours."

Flying Dutchman

Written by Brian Conway
Illustrated by Daniel Powers

Reid Brenner was the youngest and smallest sailor on the ship. It was his first voyage out to sea. The smallest sailor always had the job of night watch. Reid climbed up the ship's tallest mast.

Reid stared into the dark waves. He saw a fuzzy red flash of light. The light moved closer. Suddenly the ship rocked. A rough wave crashed against the boat. A fierce storm fell upon the ship.

Reid looked down at the sea. There, beside his ship, another ship bobbed on the waves. The ship was old. Its sails were tattered.

The crew of the strange ship looked up at him. Their eyes were gloomy. All their clothes were soaked and torn. Their faces were pale.

Lightning flashed again. Suddenly, the storm ended. The ghostly ship was gone. Reid looked for the ship. He could not see it.

The next morning, some of Reid's mates asked about the sudden storm. Reid told no one what he saw.

Later that day, Reid Brenner was struck with a terrible fever. His ship was miles from shore. There was no doctor on the ship. He could not be saved.

Sailors tell many stories of the sea. Some are true, and some are legends. One story has been told for hundreds of years. The *Flying Dutchman* was a ship that sailed the seas long ago. In 1641, this ship sailed into a terrible storm.

The captain, a proud man named Hendrick Vanderdecken, would not stop or turn his doomed ship around. The captain ordered his crew to push through the dangerous storm.

The captain and crew of the *Flying Dutchman* never reached land.

Some sailors say the *Flying Dutchman* still sails the seas today. It is said that the ship must sail through stormy waters forever.

For almost four hundred years, sailors have reported seeing the phantom ship. Often it appears from nowhere and disappears as quickly. Usually it is seen at night or during a storm.

The ship's ghostly crew may be seen working on the deck. Some sailors have claimed to see the *Flying Dutchman's* captain. They say he sadly warns them to stay away.

Any ship that crosses the *Flying Dutchman's* path is said to be doomed, too. After seeing the phantom ship, other ships have had accidents. Many sailors have gotten sick. Some have died not long after reporting a sighting.

The sea is a dangerous place. Sailors throughout history have faced storms, pirates, and diseases.

On long voyages, they tell many stories to each other. Legends of haunted ships have been told for centuries. The story of the *Flying Dutchman* has been told again and again.

It is not just an old tale of the sea. Sightings have been reported in modern times. Many people claim they have seen it.

The story of Hendrick Vanderdecken's ship is true. His ship and his crew were caught in a storm. They never made it to shore.

The reports of strange sightings are hard to ignore. The terrible tragedies that happened after sightings are also very real. But are they all related to seeing the phantom ship?

Many ships have been lost at sea. There is no way to know what happened. Lost ships leave no explanations. Their crews are never heard from again. They may have been sunk by storms. They may have crashed into rocks. Some may have crossed the path of a phantom ship.

Were the last faces those doomed sailors saw the ghostly faces of the crew and captain of the *Flying Dutchman*?

How He Left the Hotel

Based on the original story by Louisa Baldwin
Adapted by Lora Kalkman
Illustrated by Ellen Beier

After the Civil War ended, I headed to New York City. My captain was from New York. He had told me all about the city.

"Stop by the Empire Hotel, Mole," he told me when I was discharged. "I know some people there. Perhaps I can get you a job."

New York was exciting. I decided to take my captain's advice and stopped by the Empire Hotel. It was an elegant red brick building with a fancy lobby.

"Welcome," said the friendly doorman. He was dressed in a uniform with polished brass buttons and a stylish cap.

"My name's Joe," he said with a grin. I shook his hand and then introduced myself. Joe introduced me to the hotel manager.

"I spoke with your captain," the manager said. "I'd like to offer you a job. We need someone to operate the hotel elevator from two o'clock in the afternoon until twelve midnight. We'll provide wages and a room."

Like everything at the Empire Hotel, the elevator was modern and fancy. It had a decorative light inside and mirrors on the walls. It even had velvet cushions where visitors could rest during their ride.

One November, a new tenant arrived at the Empire Hotel. His name was Colonel Saxby. Colonel Saxby was also a Civil War veteran. I knew right away because he often wore his military cloak.

Colonel Saxby moved into room 210. It was on the fourth floor. Room 210 was right across from the elevator. I saw his door every time I stopped on the fourth floor.

Colonel Saxby was a kindly gentleman who kept to himself. I figured he was in his fifties. He was tall and thin, with a gray mustache and a pointy nose. His skin was pale. He had a reddish scar on one cheek. He also walked with a very slight limp.

"I took a bullet in the knee," he explained to me one day.

Sometimes, in the elevator, the colonel and I would talk a bit about the war. Even though he would talk to me, I wouldn't say he was overly friendly. That did not bother me, though.

Since I worked the elevator, I came to know everyone's routine. Colonel Saxby was especially predictable. He rode the elevator up to the fourth floor at the same time each day. He never rode it down, though. I figured he must have used the stairs.

I was proud to tell people I worked at the Empire Hotel. It was one of New York's finest. Sometimes operating the elevator grew dull, but I really enjoyed all the people.

I became good friends with a few of the other workers. Joe, the doorman, worked the same shift as I did. When it was slow in the evening, we would often talk. He told me all about his brothers in Boston. I told him about my sister in Connecticut. A lot of times we talked about the war.

Every night at midnight, I always locked the elevator. Joe generally tidied up the lobby a bit. Then, on Wednesdays, we headed to the community room for a game of cards. Helen, one of the hotel housekeepers, often joined us.

Helen was cheerful and talkative. She always kept things lively. Best of all, she generally brought us something good to eat. Her homemade soup and meat loaf sandwiches were mighty welcome after a long day.

"This is delicious," I told Helen one cold February night. She had baked an apple pie. I dare say it was the best I ever tasted.

Joe pushed his empty plate aside and thanked Helen for the meal. Then, as usual, he began shuffling his well-worn deck of cards. The three of us played until the wee hours of the morning.

The next day, I found myself watching the front door, waiting for Colonel Saxby to arrive. The colonel always rode the elevator up at three o'clock each day. In fact, I could not recall a single day when he had not been on time.

I guess there is a first time for everything, though. Colonel Saxby never did show up that day. He did not show up the next day either.

"Have you seen Colonel Saxby lately?" I finally asked Joe.

"No, Mole. I can't say that I have," he replied. "I'm told he's very ill."

At the end of my shift that night, I had just started to lock up the elevator when the call bell rang on the fourth floor. I figured it must be a visitor who did not realize the elevator stopped running at midnight.

As the clock struck twelve, I rode to the fourth floor. When I opened the elevator door, I was very surprised to see Colonel Saxby. His military cape was draped over his shoulders. I noticed his skin was even paler than usual. The man looked ill. I was really concerned about him. I wondered why he was venturing out so late at night.

"I'm glad to see you're better, sir," I said. But Colonel Saxby just looked at me with a hollow stare. Then he boarded the elevator. It was the first time I had ever given him a ride down.

When the elevator stopped in the lobby, I opened the door. Colonel Saxby, who had stood perfectly still during the ride, departed without a word.

Joe opened the door. Then Colonel Saxby walked out into the snow.

Just then, the doorbell rang. Joe opened the door. A gentleman with a black bag entered. I could tell at once he was a doctor.

"Fourth floor," he said hastily.

"I'm sorry, but the elevator stops running at midnight," I explained.

"This is a matter of life and death," said the doctor.

I did as he requested. The doctor rushed straight to room 210.

"Oh, dear," I heard the doctor sigh. "I'm afraid I'm too late. Colonel Saxby has passed away." The doctor covered Colonel Saxby's face with his sheet.

"That can't be," I said. "I took the colonel down in the elevator just a few minutes ago. Joe saw him, too. Colonel Saxby just left the hotel."

"It must have been someone else," the doctor said.

The manager asked me to take Colonel Saxby's body down in the elevator.

"I can't do that, sir," I said. "I can't take the colonel down again."

I knew I couldn't stay at the Empire Hotel any longer—not after what I'd seen. I turned in my keys and left that night. Joe, the doorman, left with me.

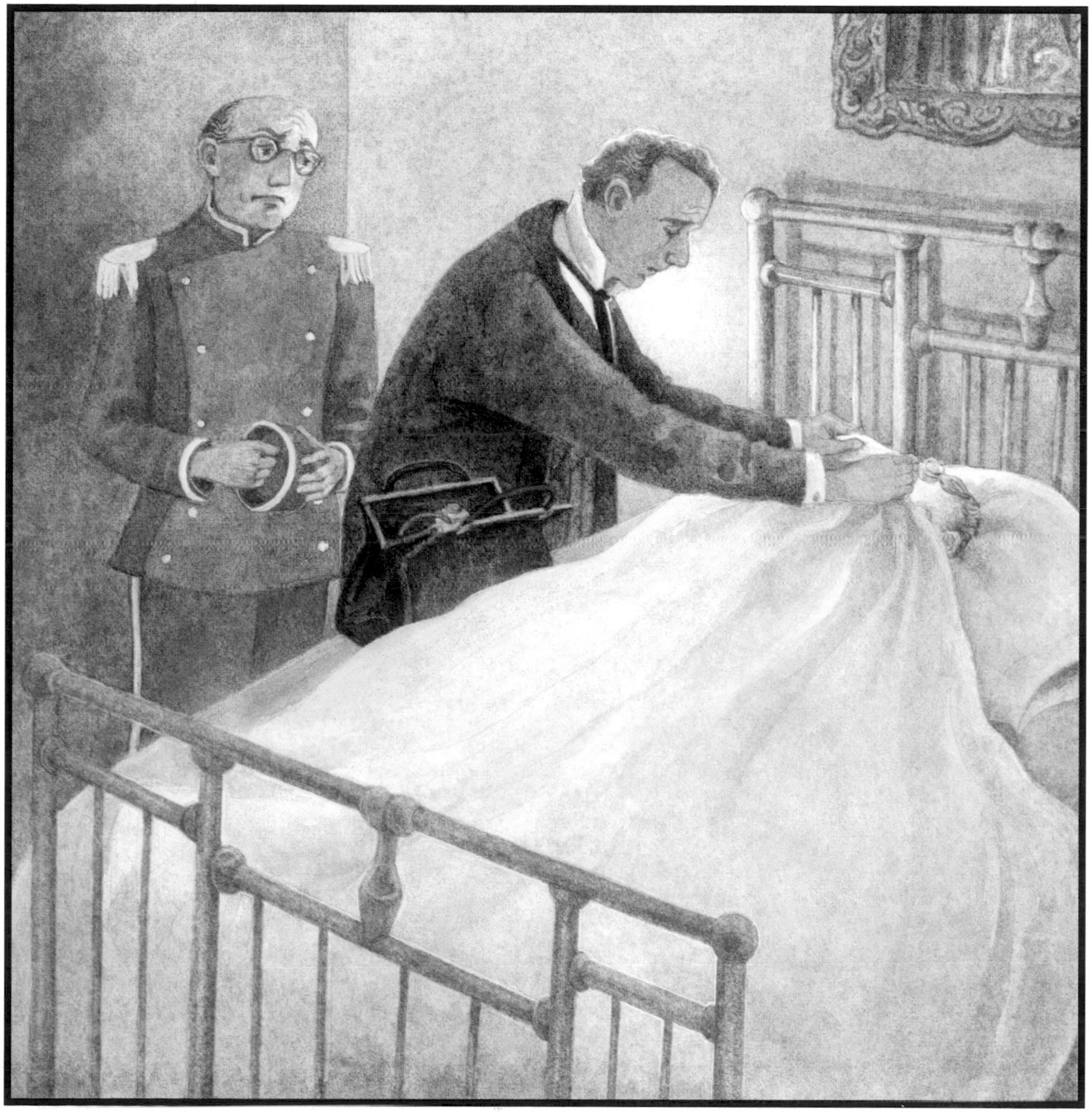

The Red Ribbon

Written by Leslie Lindecker
Illustrated by Gerardo Suzán

Bill whistled a jazzy tune. "Tonight's the night!" he thought. He strolled through Central Park on his way to meet Sally, his best girl.

There was still snow on the ground. But Bill could smell spring in the air. He jingled the engagement ring in his pocket. "A June wedding would be just right."

Bill saw Sally coming down the path towards him. He ran to her. He spun her around in his arms.

Sally squealed with delight. Bill settled Sally back down onto the park bench. He kneeled on one knee in front of her.

"Sally," Bill said, "you are the most beautiful girl I've ever met. I love you and I want you to be my wife. Will you marry me?"

Sally laughed and said, "Yes! I will marry you."

As Bill gazed lovingly at his bride-to-be, his eyes lingered on the red velvet ribbon Sally always wore around her neck.

"Why do you always wear that red ribbon?" Bill asked.

Sally said, "Bill, I must never take off my red ribbon!"

Bill smiled at Sally and left the ribbon alone.

Bill and Sally were married that June. Bill found a lovely little house in a nice neighborhood and they moved in.

Bill bought Sally many party dresses. But Sally always wore her red ribbon with each outfit. Bill thought this was odd.

Sally just smiled and said, "I must never take off my red ribbon."

After a few years, Sally found out she was going to have a baby. This news delighted Bill.

Sally talked with her friends who had babies. Bill talked with his buddies who had children. They talked together late into the night about what they had learned from everyone.

When the big day came, Sally said, "Please tell the doctor I must not take off my red ribbon!"

Bill was frustrated. But he promised Sally that he would tell the doctor.

After the baby was born, Bill gave Sally flowers.

"Thank you for the flowers, Bill," Sally said. "And thank you for telling the doctor I must not take off my red ribbon."

Bill did not understand why the red ribbon was so important.

"Do you want to hold little Billy?" Sally asked.

Bill, Sally, and little Billy lived happily for many years in the small, lovely house in the nice neighborhood.

When little Billy was a baby, he would sometimes reach for the red ribbon around his mother's neck. Sally would gently take his little hands in hers and coo at him, saying, "Mommy must never ever take off her red ribbon!"

The red ribbon had frustrated Bill for a long time. He loved Sally with all of his heart, but did not understand her need to wear the red ribbon.

After many years, Bill had an idea. "Our anniversary is coming up. I will buy Sally a beautiful necklace. She will take off that old red ribbon so she can wear the beautiful necklace!"

Their anniversary came. Bill took Sally to a fancy restaurant overlooking Central Park. They had a delicious meal.

Then Bill gave Sally a velvet box with a beautiful diamond necklace in it. She opened it, smiled, and tears came to her eyes. Bill put the necklace around her neck and started to take off the red ribbon.

Sally stopped him. She said, "I must never take off my red ribbon!" Bill sat back in his seat with a huff. He looked at Sally and shook his head.

"I may never understand," Bill said.

Sally gently placed the diamond necklace back in the velvet box and closed the lid. "It is lovely, Bill. I will treasure it always," she said. "But I must never take off my red ribbon."

"Why?" Bill asked, as he had for so many years.

Sally smiled sadly and shook her head. She did not answer him.

Late that night Bill was still awake. "I've loved Sally for more than twenty years. But she insists on wearing that horrible red ribbon around her neck. I think it's about time I found out why."

Bill got out of bed and walked around to Sally's side. Bill carefully pinched the ends of the bow on the ribbon. He began to slowly pull on the ribbon.

The bow became smaller and smaller. The loops of the bow pulled through and only a half-knot was left.

Bill slid his finger under the half-knot and tugged.

ZIP! The red ribbon gave way.

POP! Sally's head came off. It rolled right to the floor, bouncing in the moonlight!

One large tear fell from Sally's eye.

"I warned you!" she said.

Dr. Jekyll's Diary

Based on the original story by Robert Louis Stevenson
Written by Amy Adair
Illustrated by David Cooper

I am going to write everything down. If he discovers it, he'll destroy it. He wants to get rid of me, so he can live forever.

Mr. Hyde is not far. No, I fear he will come at any moment. I have been in my laboratory for three days just waiting for him.

It all started about a year ago. Back then, I had a good life in London. I was a doctor. I helped many sick people.

The night my life changed forever, my butler Poole said to me, "Dr. Jekyll, you help so many people."

I smiled and thought, "If only he knew about my other side."

I ate my dinner alone that night. Then I quickly headed down to my lab.

There was my magic formula! I had invented a liquid that could make me two different people. My good side would be one person. My bad side would be a totally different person.

I poured special powder into the glass. It turned green, then purple, and finally red. Steam rose from the glass and hung in the air like a cloud. The smell burned my nose. I held my breath. I drank it in one gulp.

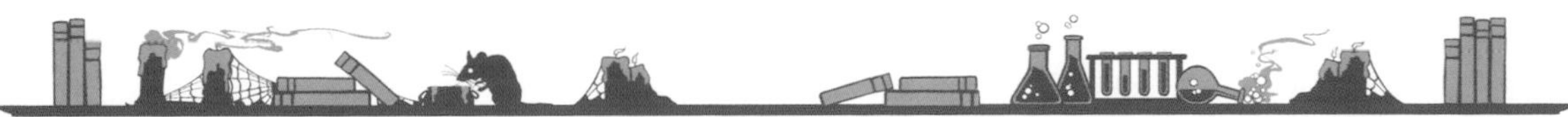

Oh! The pain! My body shook. I cried out. Then the pain stopped.

I felt strange. I looked in the mirror.

I gasped! The eyes staring back at me were not Dr. Jekyll's wise brown eyes. The eyes in the mirror were gray and beady. My hair was wild. My teeth were crooked and pointy. I was ugly.

But I liked the new me. I named this new face Mr. Edward Hyde.

I went out the back door. I saw a horse and carriage on the side of the street.

I climbed in and yelled, "Take me to Soho!"

"Yes, sir," the driver said.

I spit out the window. I yelled at people on the street. Oh, how free I felt!

Before I knew it the driver called, "This is Soho, sir."

I jumped out and asked, "Do you want your money?"

"Yes, sir," the driver answered.

Instead of paying the driver, I swatted his horse with my cane and yelled, "Yah! Away! Yah!" The frightened horse galloped wildly down the street.

I laughed as I heard the driver yell, "Steady, boy! Steady!"

Soon it was morning. I hurried home. I snuck down to my lab and drank my magic formula. I was Dr. Jekyll again.

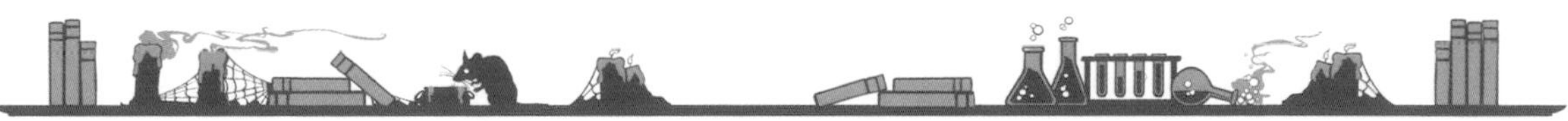

That morning, I opened my office late. I went shopping for clothes that would fit Mr. Hyde. For weeks, I was Mr. Hyde by night and Dr. Jekyll by day.

One night, Poole said to me, "Sir, Mr. Utterson is here to see you. He is waiting in the study."

Mr. Utterson looked worried. "Good evening, Dr. Jekyll," he said.

"Good evening," I said. "To what do I owe this visit?"

"Dr. Jekyll, we've been friends for a long time," Mr. Utterson said. "I just wanted to see if anything is wrong."

"Nothing is wrong," I answered.

I thought I saw Poole hiding in the shadows listening to our conversation. I wondered what they knew.

"You have not been yourself lately," Mr. Utterson said. "This new friend of yours, Mr. Hyde, seems to be trouble. Why would you ever want to be friends with the likes of him?"

Oh! If only Mr. Utterson knew the truth! But I could not tell him.

"Mr. Utterson, thank you for your concern," I said. "You are a dear friend of mine. Mr. Hyde may be an interesting character, but I can assure you there is nothing to raise concern. Please excuse me. I have work to do in my lab."

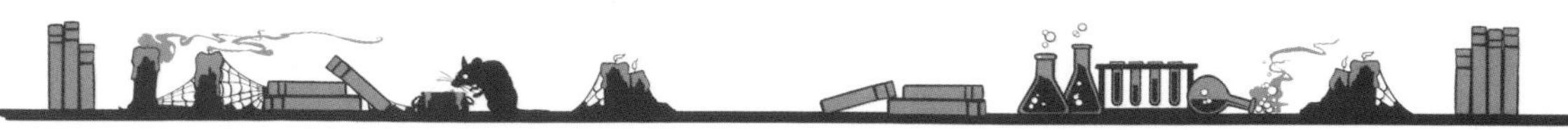

I went down to the lab and quickly drank my magic formula.

This time I only drank half a glass, but I changed into Mr. Hyde even faster.

I snuck out the back door and tried to stay hidden in the shadows. But I saw Poole and Mr. Utterson watching me from the window.

I wandered up and down the streets of London. When the sun started to rise, I began to walk back to my house.

That was when all the trouble started. To be honest, I did not even see her. I slammed into a little child. I knocked her straight to the ground with a thud.

I did not care about the girl. I yelled, "Get out of my way, child!"

I kept walking. I did not look back. Then I felt a hand on my shoulder.

"Hey, you!" said a stern voice. "Did you knock that child over?"

"So what if I did?" I replied. I ran away.

"Police! Police!" cried the man.

A police officer chased me.

"You there! Stop!" he yelled, as he grabbed his whistle. Tooot! Tooot!

I ran. Faster and faster and faster! If Mr. Hyde went to jail so would the good Dr. Jekyll. I did not look back. I ran straight to my house and into the lab. I slammed the door. I drank a glass of my magic formula. Nothing happened.

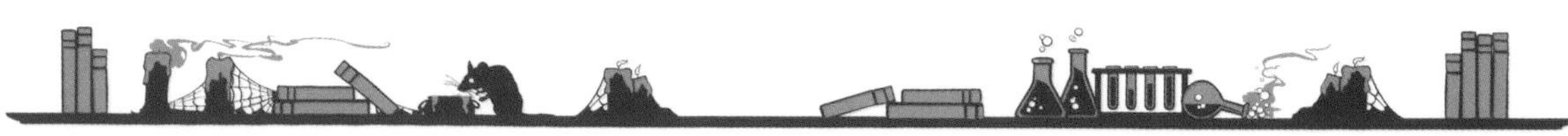

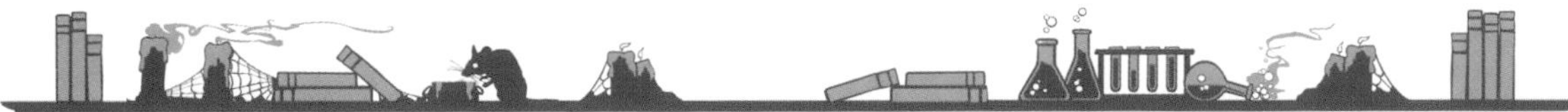

I drank another glass. Still nothing happened. Finally after four full glasses of the magic formula, I turned back into the good Dr. Jekyll.

I knew that Mr. Hyde could get Dr. Jekyll into trouble. So I did the only thing that I could. I put away Mr. Hyde's clothes.

I locked away my magic formula. It was for the best, because I was running out of the special powder and could not find any as strong.

I could not get Mr. Hyde out of my head. This went on for months.

But yesterday morning changed everything. I woke with a start. My knuckles were thick like knots, and my hands looked like claws. I glanced at the mirror. I knew whose face I would see — Mr. Hyde's.

Imagine my terror! I had not swallowed any magic formula! Not one single drop! I ran out of my bedroom and down to my lab.

I drank one glass of my magic formula. Nothing happened. Finally! After drinking five glasses, I changed back into Dr. Jekyll.

I went back to work. An hour later, my head began to ache. I was seeing one of my older patients. "Doctor," he said. "Is something wrong?"

I could not speak. I dropped his medical chart. I ran out of the office and down towards my lab. Before I made it to my lab, I changed into Mr. Hyde.

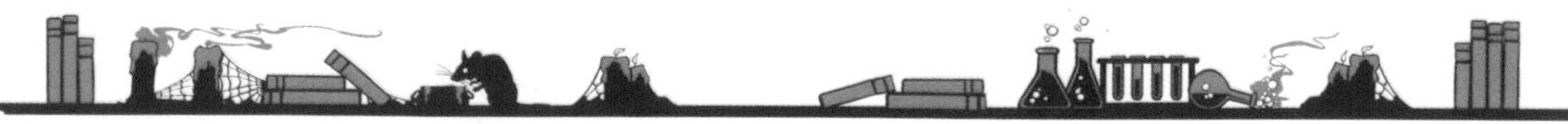

I drank the last six glasses of my magic formula. I don't have any more. I have just a short time left. I am writing so everyone will know the horrible truth that I, Dr. Jekyll, am also Mr. Hyde.

I'm just waiting for Mr. Hyde to show his ugly face again. I am afraid to shut my eyes to sleep. He'll come if I do. He can come by himself now. He does not need any magic formula. He is much stronger than Dr. Jekyll.

I can hear Poole upstairs as I write this. I hear other people, too.

I hear stomp, stomp, stomp, down the steps. The footsteps are getting closer! Closer! Closer! They are just outside my door.

They cannot meet Mr. Hyde. He could hurt them!

I can hear Poole calling to me. "Dr. Jekyll are you in there?"

"Go away!" I yell back. Perhaps if he reads this diary he'll understand.

"We only want to help!" says another voice. Oh, no! It is Mr. Utterson, too.

"Go away! Go away! Why don't you listen to me?" My head aches.

Bang! Bang! Bang! Axes. I hear axes slashing at the door.

What can I do? Bang! Bang! They are almost in!

Mr. Hyde is very near. He'll be here any minute...

The Loch Ness Monster

Written by Brian Conway
Illustrated by Aaron Boyd

Loch Ness is a deep lake in Scotland. The lake is so dark, it is very hard to see anything underwater. But one girl saw something that she will never forget. In 1960, Alice Logan visited Loch Ness for a day of sailing with her parents.

She had heard stories about a sea monster that lived in the lake. It had a long neck and even had a nickname. People called the creature "Nessie." They said it lived deep below the surface of the lake.

"Alice, why don't you put away those binoculars and play?" her father asked.

"I am going to get proof that Nessie is real," she explained.

Alice looked down into the water. She thought she saw something move. She leaned over the edge of the boat and fell into the cold water.

For a few seconds, she was underwater. It was dark, but she could see a shape right in front of her. It was a swimming beast, with a long neck and a tiny head. It had to be Nessie!

Just then, Alice's life preserver lifted her back to the surface. She rubbed the water from her eyes and searched the murky water again. But the strange creature was gone.

Even though so many people have seen and even photographed the Loch Ness Monster, there are still many questions about the creature. Is there only one monster? Does Nessie have a family? If it really exists, where did it come from? What kind of creature is Nessie?

Scientists have many ideas. Some think Nessie could be a strange type of giant eel. Maybe it is a type of whale or seal that no one has ever seen before.

Another theory is that Nessie is a relative of a prehistoric fish called the plesiosaur. Scientists always thought the last plesiosaur died millions of years ago. But maybe Nessie's relatives have lived in the lake for all these years.

Scientists think there might be a lot of mysterious creatures living in deep lakes all around the world. People have seen strange sea monsters in New York, Canada, and Russia. Could these be Nessie's relatives?

Will anyone ever be able to prove that the Loch Ness Monster exists? If the creature exists, it knows how to hide well. It has been hiding from people for hundreds of years.

It is possible that Nessie and all of her relatives have lived in Loch Ness for millions of years. Will Nessie or one of her family members ever reveal themselves to us?

Stories about the Loch Ness Monster go back hundreds of years. The ancient Scottish people who lived near the lake told tales about the creature.

In 1933, more than ninety people said they saw the Loch Ness Monster. Many stories appeared in newspapers all over the world.

Altogether, more than four thousand people have reported that they saw something unusual in the waters of Loch Ness. The stories are hard to prove because it is so hard to search in the dark lake.

Loch Ness is a long, narrow lake. It is almost like a wide river, but it is also very deep. Diving is difficult in the lake because it is so dark. The water is full of tiny floating pieces of brown coal.

Scientists have to use machines to search the mysterious waters. Not even the most expensive cameras, submarines, and other devices could find Nessie. The rocky bottom of the deep lake makes it easy for a clever sea beast to hide.

Some scientists took photographs in the lake. The photos show an animal that is almost as big as a school bus. The beast has a wide body, fins, a skinny neck, and a tail.

The photographs are real, but many of them are cloudy or unclear. There is still no proof that Nessie exists.

Even though so many people have seen and even photographed the Loch Ness Monster, there are still many questions about the creature. Is there only one monster? Does Nessie have a family? If it really exists, where did it come from? What kind of creature is Nessie?

Scientists have many ideas. Some think Nessie could be a strange type of giant eel. Maybe it is a type of whale or seal that no one has ever seen before.

Another theory is that Nessie is a relative of a prehistoric fish called the plesiosaur. Scientists always thought the last plesiosaur died millions of years ago. But maybe Nessie's relatives have lived in the lake for all these years.

Scientists think there might be a lot of mysterious creatures living in deep lakes all around the world. People have seen strange sea monsters in New York, Canada, and Russia. Could these be Nessie's relatives?

Will anyone ever be able to prove that the Loch Ness Monster exists? If the creature exists, it knows how to hide well. It has been hiding from people for hundreds of years.

It is possible that Nessie and all of her relatives have lived in Loch Ness for millions of years. Will Nessie or one of her family members ever reveal themselves to us?

The Lighthouse

Written by Renee Deshommes
Illustrated by Laurie Harden

Jack was a writer who moved to a seaside town. He traveled around the coast to write stories about the people who lived there. He did not know that he would soon have his own story to tell.

After settling into his new home by the sea, Jack decided that he needed some artwork. He had heard about an old man who ran a gallery in town. Jack woke up early one morning and walked to the gallery.

"Good morning," Jack said, as he opened the gallery door. He shook the old man's hand. Jack introduced himself, then began looking at the paintings.

The old man had an assortment of paintings. There were scenes of flowery meadows, city skylines, and desert landscapes. But Jack kept coming back to a painting of a lighthouse. It reminded him of the lighthouse at the edge of town.

"What a perfect picture for my wall," he said. "I'll take this one."

"I hope you have the perfect place for this painting," the old man said. He wrapped the painting in brown paper.

Jack paid the old man and walked home with the painting under his arm. He could not wait to find the perfect place to hang it.

That afternoon, Jack found a place above his mantel. He hammered a nail into the wall and hung the picture. Jack sat back to see if it was straight.

"This is perfect," thought Jack. "I can look out my window and see the sea. And I can look above the mantel and see the lighthouse. What inspiration!"

That evening, Jack sat down to read over some notes from the day before. He had been interviewing a young woman. Her grandfather had run the lighthouse years earlier. The young woman told many stories about her grandfather. He had loved the sea so much that he wanted to be buried there.

Jack suddenly looked up from his notes. He thought he saw shadows moving across the dark room. Jack got up and walked down the hall. He saw the shadow again! This time he caught a glimpse of a ghostly old man.

Jack shivered in the darkness. He rubbed his eyes.

"Perhaps I'm just tired," he thought. "My eyes must be playing tricks on me." Jack turned out the light and went to bed.

That night, he dreamed about the lighthouse in his new painting. Jack was standing on its platform and looking out to sea. He saw an old man sitting alone inside the lighthouse.

The man seemed very sad. Jack tried to speak to him. Then Jack woke up.

The next morning, Jack felt like he had to move the painting. He did not know why he felt that way. He just did.

He looked around his house for the perfect place. He decided the best place for the painting was right above his desk in the den. "This will inspire me to write my newest story," thought Jack.

That evening, after a quiet dinner, Jack sat down at his desk to work. He was reading a book about lighthouses when a strange feeling came over him. He felt very cold. Jack shivered as he turned the pages.

Then in the corner, Jack saw the shadow again. This time, Jack was sure it was an old man. The shadow paced back and forth in the room. Jack could tell the man was sad and restless.

Jack looked around the room. He wondered where the shadow was coming from. When he turned around, the shadow was gone.

Jack was very puzzled. He began thinking about the painting. "Could that be why the shadow is here?" he wondered. "Perhaps I have not found the perfect place for it."

Jack went to bed that night thinking about the painting and the ghostly shadows. He tossed and turned throughout the night.

In the early morning, Jack finally fell asleep. He had a dream about the old lighthouse again.

This time, the old man was looking out the window of the lighthouse. He was staring at the sea and watching the gulls dip and dive. The old man looked so happy!

Jack awoke with a start. He knew exactly what he must do.

Jack jumped out of bed and quickly got dressed. He took the painting down and carried it into his living room.

Then he found the perfect place for the painting. It was directly across from his biggest window. Jack loved sitting in front of this window himself. He would watch the waves breaking on the rocks as the sun rose each morning.

Jack hammered a nail into the wall. Then he carefully hung the painting. He stepped back to see if it was straight. Then he turned around to look at the sea. "Yes!" he exclaimed. "This is definitely the perfect place."

That night, as Jack worked, he waited for the ghostly shadow to appear. But it never did. The shadow did not appear the next night or the night after that.

Jack noticed that a certain sense of peace and calm had come over his house. He stopped dreaming about the old man and the lighthouse, too.

Soon after the strange shadow had disappeared, Jack started working on a new project. He was writing a story about the painting and the ghostly shadow.

Jack decided to start at the beginning. He described how he had found the little house by the sea. He wrote about meeting the old man at the gallery and how he chose the painting of the lighthouse. Then he came to the part about the warning from the owner of the gallery. "I hope you have the perfect place for this painting," he had said.

The old man's comment made Jack wonder. "Did he know all along that the painting was haunted?" Jack thought. "Did he know the painting belonged near the sea?"

Jack decided to take a break from his writing. He got up from his desk and walked over to the painting.

Jack grabbed a cloth and dusted the wooden frame. Then he stopped to look at the picture.

Jack noticed something he had never seen before. A man was standing on the platform of the lighthouse. He was looking out to sea.

"This man looks almost like the shadow," Jack thought.

Then he realized something else. It was the same man from his dreams!

Night Coach

Based on the original story by Amelia Edwards
Adapted by Lora Kalkman
Illustrated by Jeffrey Ebbeler

Orange kicked the dusty, dry dirt with the toe of his leather boot. He cupped his hand to his mouth. "Gypsy," he called to his horse. "Gypsy, come back here!" Orange knew Gypsy was long gone.

"That horse! She sure gets spooked a lot," the cowboy said. Orange took off his brown ten-gallon hat. The sun was still hot, even though it had begun its descent behind the horizon. Night would soon fall upon the desert.

Orange had been riding through the desert to see his brother, Pete. Then all of a sudden, something startled Gypsy.

"Musta been a rattler," Orange thought. He had not seen one, though. Whatever it was, it sure scared Gypsy. She reared up and flung Orange from her back. Now Orange was stranded and did not know what to do next.

He surveyed the landscape. He saw a whole lot of sand.

Much to his surprise, Orange spotted a tiny cabin. A small trail of smoke rose from the chimney. Orange could tell the cabin was quite a ways away, but the evening air was growing brisk. He knew that temperatures in the desert dropped way down at night, so he started walking.

It was plenty dark when Orange finally made it to the cabin. But he could still see the dim light inside. He rapped at the door.

An old man, stout and balding, opened the door a crack. "Can I help you?" he asked cautiously.

"Why, yes sir. I hope so, sir," Orange said. He removed his hat politely. "Seems my horse got spooked and left me stranded here. I was hopin' you might be kind enough to give me shelter for the night."

"Come in," the man said. "I suppose you're hungry." He walked over to his kitchen and pulled some cans from a small pantry. "You're welcome to these," he offered. Then he poured Orange a cup of coffee.

While enjoying a supper of beans and stew, Orange looked around the cabin. It was filled with books and papers. A telescope rested on a nearby table.

"It's not too late to catch the night coach into town," the man offered, while Orange ate. "You could buy a new horse in the morning."

"Really?" Orange asked.

"You just need to walk out to Red Rock Hollow," the old man showed Orange on a map. "That's where there's an opening in the rocks big enough for a coach to pass. It's the most direct route through the valley."

Orange thanked the old man for the suggestion. "And thank you for this fine meal, too," he added. Then Orange grabbed his hat and set off.

Orange walked alongside rock formations, which served as his guide. He immediately noticed that the temperature had fallen.

"It's downright cold out here," Orange declared, as he made his way towards Red Rock Hollow. Something seemed eerie.

"Maybe Gypsy had the right idea," he thought, shivering.

Orange rounded a bend and saw Red Rock Hollow before him. Suddenly, he noticed two tiny, dim lights shining through the hollow. The lights were steadily growing bigger and brighter.

Excitedly, Orange realized it must be the night coach. He jumped out into its path and shouted, waving his hands. Sure enough, the coach stopped.

Now, Orange had seen a lot of coaches in his day, but he had never seen one like this! It was black from top to bottom. A jet black horse wearing a giant black plume pulled it. The driver, who had not said a word, was draped in a heavy black cloak.

"Well, this is mighty strange," Orange thought to himself. But he went ahead and hopped inside anyway.

Orange did not feel comfortable sitting inside the eerie coach. But before long, the black horse was galloping at full speed. Its hooves thundered across the desert floor.

"I wonder why the hurry," Orange thought.

Orange decided he better say something to the driver. He leaned right out the window.

"Evenin' my good man," he shouted. "I thank you kindly for the ride. How long will it take us to get to town?"

He waited for the reply, but the driver said nothing.

"It shouldn't take too long at this pace," Orange continued. There was a big lump in his throat. He felt uneasy. Something was definitely not right. The coach sped on into the night.

"Perhaps you could just let me off right here," Orange called to the driver. "I believe I may be on the wrong coach."

He was relieved when the driver finally turned around. But relief soon turned to horror. The driver had no face!

Orange's eyes grew wide. "Now I *know* I'm on the wrong coach!" he said. Out of sheer terror, he closed his eyes and jumped.

When Orange woke up, he discovered he was in a bed. His brother, Pete, was there, as well as Pete's wife and a doctor.

"Orange!" Pete said. "We're gonna have to change your name. Your hair done turned pure white! Like you seen a ghost or something."

"H-h-how did I get here?" Orange stammered. He was still in a bit of shock from his ride.

"Why, the night coachman, of course," Pete said matter-of-factly.

Orange began to shudder. It was all coming back to him now. He could still see the black coach and horses. He did not even want to think about the driver who did not have a face.

"Yes, sir," Pete continued. "Said he saw ya lying in the desert, flat on your face. He stopped to see if you was alright and brung you on here. But don't you worry none," Pete patted Orange's shoulder. "We've arranged to have another coach take you on home."

"No! No coaches!" Orange blurted out. "A horse'll suit me fine. Yes, just find me a horse, would ya, Pete?"

"Sure, brother," Pete replied.

Orange thought for a moment. "And make sure it's not black!"

Houdini's Great Escape

Written by Brian Conway
Illustrated by Allan Eitzen

Harry Houdini was probably the most famous magician of all time. People especially loved Harry Houdini's great escape tricks. He was famous for putting himself in great danger and escaping just in time.

Houdini's assistants once wrapped him tightly in heavy chains. They locked the chains together and lowered him into a large pool of water.

People in the audience could see through a window in the side of the tank. Houdini held his breath for a long time. Just when the audience thought he would drown, he escaped! He wiggled out of the chains, floated to the surface, and took a deep breath. The crowd cheered.

Houdini performed hundreds of death-defying tricks like this one. But his most famous trick was one he did from the grave—after he was already dead!

Houdini promised his wife, Bess, he would contact her from beyond the grave. With his last breaths, Houdini whispered a secret message to Bess. The message contained ten words. Only she would know the coded message. This way, she would know it was really Harry speaking to her from beyond the grave.

On Halloween night, 1926, Harry Houdini died.

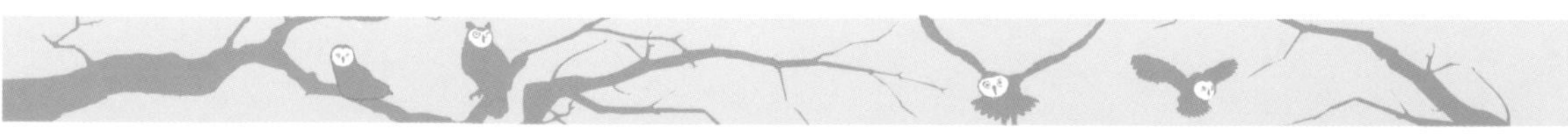

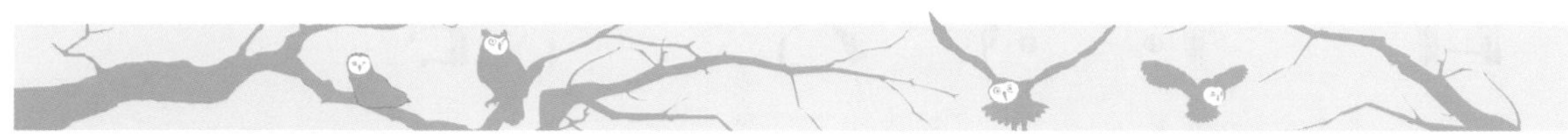

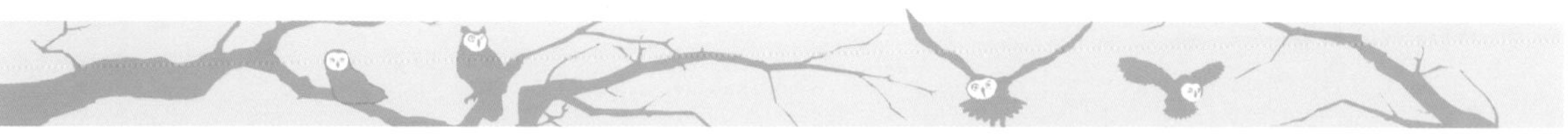

Bess Houdini saw her husband do many spectacular tricks before his death. She believed he would find a way to contact her and give her a message.

She kept a candle burning near a picture of her husband. Each year she held a séance on Halloween. A séance is when a group of living people try to talk to the spirits of people who have died.

In 1929, a man named Arthur Ford came to the séance on Halloween. He said he was a medium. A medium is a person who speaks all the words that spirits want him to say.

Ford held another candle in front of him. He closed his eyes and began to whisper and hum. His voice changed suddenly.

"Hello, Bess," Ford said in a very strange voice. The voice sounded just like Harry's voice, but this voice was far away. A cold breeze came through the open window and blew out a nearby candle. The table shook. Then Ford slowly said ten words: "Rosabelle...answer...tell...pray...answer...look...tell...answer...answer...tell..."

These were the exact words Houdini whispered to his wife on Halloween three years earlier. Bess was amazed. She believed her husband had reached out to her from beyond the grave.

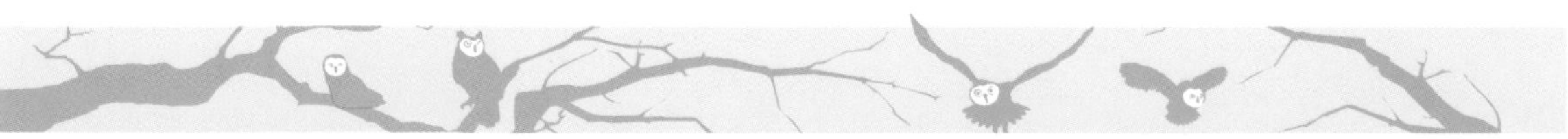

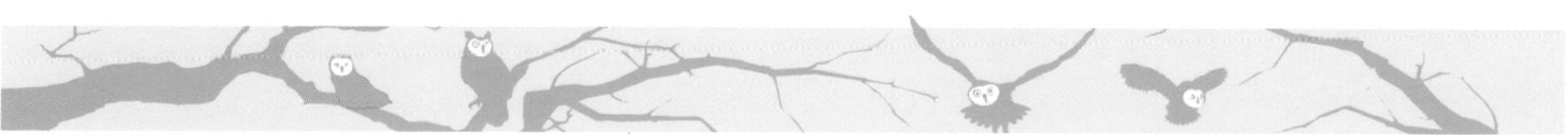

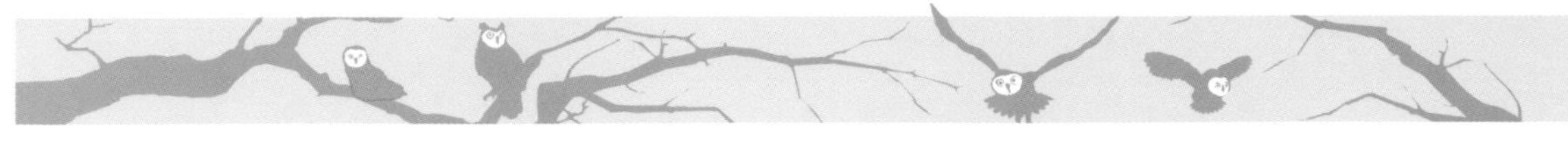

Did Houdini really figure out a way to speak to his wife from the spirit world? Or was the séance a hoax? If Arthur Ford was a fake, how did he know Houdini's message?

The words in the message were a special code for letters of the alphabet. Each word stood for a different letter in the alphabet. In their secret code the letters spelled the word, "BELIEVE."

In 1929, newspapers printed many articles about the séance. Even though Houdini's message said to "BELIEVE," many people did not believe it was real.

One newspaper article said Bess Houdini and Arthur Ford planned the séance as a show to make money. Some believed that Ford and Bess Houdini made a deal. If she told him Harry Houdini's secret message, he would share some of his riches with her. In fact, Ford became quite famous after the séance.

Other people believed, and still believe, that Harry's spirit really did speak to Bess. Even today, people hold séances on Halloween night every year. They try to talk to Houdini.

They want Houdini's spirit to reveal how he did such an amazing trick. They believe that if anyone could have escaped death, it would be Harry Houdini, the greatest escape artist of all time.

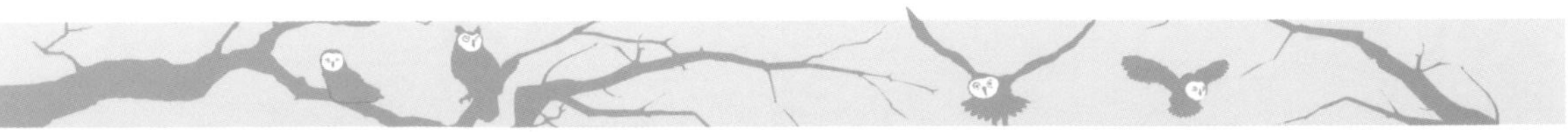

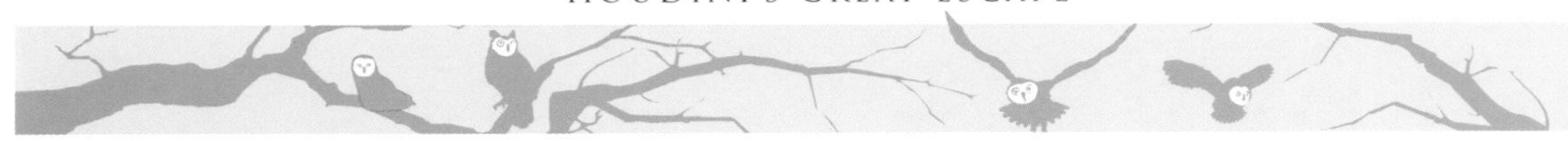

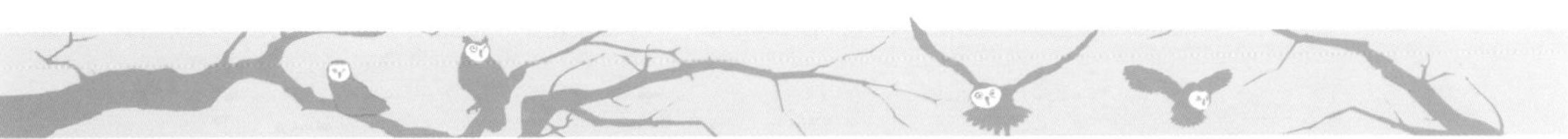

The Selkie Child

Written by Amy Adair
Illustrated by Beatriz Helena Ramos

Martin threw his net over the side of his fishing boat. It fanned out like a giant spiderweb. As he waited for his net to fill with fish, he watched seals on the rocks. Martin pulled his net in, docked his boat, and began to walk home. When he passed the rocks, he noticed the seals had left a small bundle.

"It's a baby girl!" Martin cried. Next to the baby was a seal's skin.

"This must be a Selkie baby," whispered Martin. He had heard fishermen tell tales about beautiful creatures called Selkies. Selkies could change from a seal to a human by shedding their skin.

Martin cradled the baby in one arm and tucked the seal skin under his coat and ran home.

He opened the door and yelled to his wife, "Sela! The sea gave us a baby."

Sela scooped the baby out of Martin's arms and said, "She's beautiful."

"Let's name her Morgan," Martin said. "It means a 'gift from the sea.'"

Martin did not tell Sela that Morgan was a Selkie child and might want to return to the sea when she grew up. Instead, he locked the little seal skin in a trunk in the attic.

Morgan grew up to be a beautiful child. Sela and Morgan spent the days swimming while Martin fished. Martin watched Morgan from his boat.

"She's almost as good a swimmer as her mother," Martin said. "I will tell Sela the truth about Morgan as soon as I return from my long fishing trip."

The day Martin left for his trip, a storm came up the coast.

Morgan stared out the kitchen window. "I'd like to go swimming."

"You cannot swim during a storm," Sela said. "It's too dangerous."

"I'm sure it's peaceful under the waves," Morgan said.

The next morning, Sela and Morgan found pieces of Martin's boat washed up on the beach. Martin never came home.

That night, another storm came up the coast. When Sela drifted off to sleep she heard a familiar voice whisper, "I can't rest until I tell you the truth!"

"Morgan!" Sela whispered with fright. She ran to Morgan's room. A bolt of lightning lit it up. The bed was empty. Sela searched every room.

When Sela stopped in front of the attic door, the doorknob slowly turned.

Trembling, she watched as the door creaked open. She whispered, "Morgan! Morgan! Are you in here?"

There was no answer, so she quickly shut the door and locked it.

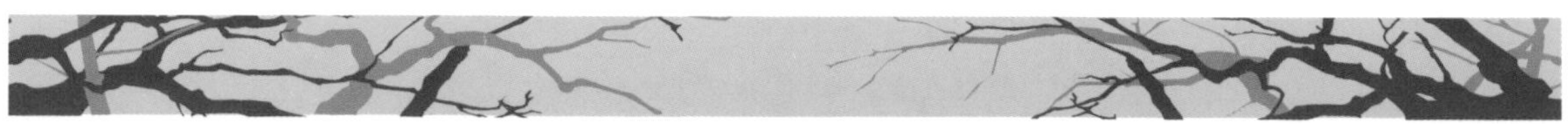

"Morgan!" Sela cried. The wind was getting stronger. Sela ran down the steps. She peered through the kitchen window and saw Morgan standing on the rocks near the water.

Sela stumbled through the heavy wet sand on the beach. Thick storm clouds covered the moon.

"Mama," Morgan said. "Do you ever feel like you don't belong here?"

Sela shook her head and said, "I belong here with you."

Morgan and Sela walked back up to the house. When Sela went to the pantry to get Morgan a towel, she heard *stomp, stomp, stomp* above her.

"Someone is upstairs," Sela gasped.

Creeaakk! Sela knew the attic door was opening.

Sela lit a candle. They tiptoed up the steps. The attic door was open.

"Stay here," Sela told Morgan. Sela stepped inside.

"Mama!" Morgan cried. She peeked inside the attic.

Sela stood very still. Something moved.

A trunk suddenly slid towards her. She reached down and opened it.

Sela felt something cold and wet inside the trunk. She held it up. She saw a tiny seal's skin.

"Come with me!" Sela said. She grabbed Morgan's trembling hand and led her down three flights of steps to the basement.

Sela moved a pile of boxes and found a large chest.

"I hid this here years ago," Sela explained. She pulled out a seal's skin.

"What is it?" Morgan whispered.

"It's a seal's skin," Sela answered. "I'm a Selkie."

"This is your seal skin," Sela showed Morgan the smaller skin. "Your father must have known you were a Selkie. He just didn't know how to tell me."

Sela explained how she had fallen in love with Morgan's father when she was young. She hid her seal skin from him and gave up her seal life. "I always longed for the sea," Sela said to Morgan, "but I could never leave you. Tonight you will see just how peaceful it is under the waves."

Sela and Morgan ran to the beach and slipped into their seal skins. As they swam, they saw a familiar boat drifting along with the tide.

"Look, Mama," Morgan whispered. "It looks like Papa's boat."

Sela looked up and saw the ghostly figure of her husband standing on the boat's deck. A wave splashed over Sela and Morgan. When they wiped the water out of their eyes, the boat was gone.

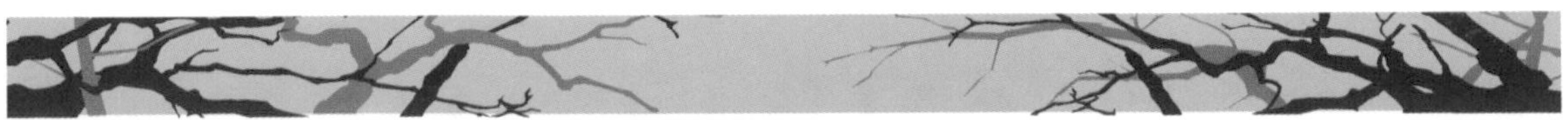

Ghost Cave

Written by Lisa Harkrader
Illustrated by Kathleen Estes

Riley counted his workers. Then he yelled, “Line up, men!” Riley was the foreman of a road construction crew. He had to make sure everyone reported for work. This morning he counted an extra worker, a teenage boy.

The boy stepped forward. “My name’s Tate. I’m here for the job.”

Riley studied the boy. He did not look healthy. He was skinny and pale.

“I can’t have kids running around getting hurt,” Riley said.

“I won’t get hurt, sir,” said Tate. “I can do the work of three men.”

Tate grasped the bumper of Riley’s truck with one hand. He took a deep breath and lifted the front of the truck off the ground. He took another breath and lifted it over his head.

Riley laughed. “Okay, son. You’ve got the job.”

Tate worked hard all day. He never took a break. He did not stop for lunch. At the end of the day, Riley handed out pay envelopes to all the men. Tate put the envelope in his pocket and walked towards town.

The next morning, Tate reported early for work. He worked very hard all day, collected his pay envelope, then set off for home.

On Saturday, Riley went into town for a haircut and a shave.

"So how's the work coming along?" the barber asked.

"Fine, fine," said Riley. "We've gotten more road dug the last few days than we have all summer."

The barber raised his eyebrows. "Is that so? What's causing your men to work so much faster all of a sudden?"

"It's not the men," said Riley. "It's a boy. I've got a new worker on the crew. He can't be more than fifteen or sixteen. Maybe you know him. His name's Tate."

"Oh, yes." The barber nodded. "Tate. He's an odd one, he is. And you're right—he doesn't look older than sixteen. But he has to be at least twenty. Lived here all his life."

"You think that boy is twenty?" Riley asked.

"Why, yes," said the barber. "But the funny thing is, he doesn't seem to get any older. Once he got to be a teenager, he just stopped aging. He's even worn the same clothes for the last five or six years, and he never needs a haircut."

Riley frowned. "That's very strange. Think I should have a talk with him?"

"No, leave him be," said the barber. "He's a good boy. He works hard. He has to. His mama's sickly, and she needs him."

Riley left the barber shop. Outside he saw two women, Mrs. Malloy and Mrs. Winslow, chatting in front of the dress shop.

"Good day, ladies," he said.

But the women were too involved in their conversation to notice him.

"The poor boy will miss his mama," Mrs. Winslow was saying.

"Poor Tate," said Mrs. Malloy.

"Tate?" Riley wheeled around. "Pardon me. I don't mean to eavesdrop, but were you just talking about a thin, fair-haired boy named Tate?"

"Yes. His mother passed away this morning," said Mrs. Malloy.

"I'm sorry to hear that," said Riley.

"She's been sick for a very long time," said Mrs. Winslow. "Last week she took a turn for the worse. She kept getting weaker and weaker."

Mrs. Malloy nodded. "It's a blessing, really, that the poor old lady no longer has to suffer."

"But Tate will be heartbroken," said Mrs. Winslow.

"He adored his mother," said Mrs. Malloy. "He spent all his time caring for her. It's as if he had no other purpose in life. I don't know what will become of the poor boy now."

Suddenly, Mrs. Malloy's son came running up. "Mama, Mama!" the boy shrieked. "You'll never guess what we saw."

"Slow down, Jimmy," said Mrs. Malloy. "Tell me what happened."

Jimmy took a deep breath. "We were playing near the creek. Tate walked by. He looked funny, he was even paler than usual. I could see right through him."

"Jimmy!" said Mrs. Malloy. "Don't make up stories."

"I'm not," said Jimmy. "I tried to talk to him. But Tate walked past like he didn't hear me."

"Probably thinking about his mother," said Mrs. Winslow.

"We followed him," Jimmy said. "He went out past the old mill and down to the creek. Then he walked right into the ground."

"Jimmy!" said Mrs. Malloy.

"It's true," said Jimmy. "It was a cave. I never even knew it was there. Tate got paler and paler as he walked inside. Then he just disappeared. I've got to catch up with the other kids. They went to tell the sheriff." Jimmy raced down the street.

Riley laughed. "He has an active imagination. Tate is certainly pale, but I don't think he could actually disappear."

On Monday morning, Tate did not come to work. It was not like Tate to not show up for work. Then Riley remembered Jimmy's story.

Riley put the crew to work, then set out down the road past the old mill. He saw that the sheriff had gotten to the cave before him.

"I came to see if Tate was okay," Riley told the sheriff.

"You're too late." The sheriff pointed inside the cave.

There, right in the middle of the cave, was a skeleton. Tate's clothes and work boots were rotting in a heap around the brittle bones.

"That can't be Tate," said Riley. "He was working for me last week."

The sheriff nodded. "I've seen him around town, too. I'd say this skeleton has been here about five years. Funny thing is, five years ago is just about the time Tate stopped getting older. He started looking paler and skinnier. I found this in his pocket." The sheriff unfolded a piece of paper. "It's his mother's grocery bill. Paid in full. Tate always took good care of her."

"And he kept taking care of her even after he was dead," said Riley.

He pointed to the date on the paper. Tate had paid the bill on Saturday, the very day his mother died. "I guess he can stop taking care of his mother now," said Riley.

Interview With Dr. Frankenstein

Based on the original story by Mary Shelley
Adapted by Brian Conway
Illustrated by Fabricio Vanden Broeck

There once was a man named Dr. Victor Frankenstein. He created a big monster, but then the monster ran away. Dr. Frankenstein looked all over the world for his monster.

Dr. Frankenstein visited his friend, Henry Clerval. Clerval wanted to know what happened. Clerval asked Dr. Frankenstein many questions.

"I tried to create a man," Dr. Frankenstein said, "but I created a monster."

Dr. Frankenstein worked very hard on this experiment. He tried to create a living person out of many parts of lifeless bodies. He sewed together body parts that he found in graveyards. Finally, the creature came to life!

The man he made was eight feet tall. He had stitches sewn around his pale skin. He could only grunt and growl like a wild animal, but he was alive!

"The creature opened his eyes and looked at me," Dr. Frankenstein said. "I knew right away that I had made a terrible mistake."

The monster groaned very loudly. The monster reached out with his huge hands. Dr. Frankenstein was afraid of the monster he created. Dr. Frankenstein ran away from his lab. When he returned the next day, the monster was gone.

"What happened next?" asked Clerval.

"I was afraid," said Dr. Frankenstein. "I shouldn't have left the creature alone in the lab. It was not ready to be out in the world. And the world will never be ready to accept such a frightening creature."

"Where did the monster go?" Clerval asked.

"I have been looking for him," said Dr. Frankenstein. "During my search, I have talked to many people who saw the monster."

Dr. Frankenstein told Clerval about a man who saw the monster in the woods near the laboratory. The monster saw the man's campfire. The simple monster liked the light and warmth of the fire. The man was frightened by the monster. He ran to the village and told everyone what he saw.

"What did the villagers do?" Clerval wanted to know.

"They went back to the woods with torches and clubs," Dr. Frankenstein said. "They were afraid of the monster. They did not know that the monster was also afraid of them."

The creature began to growl angrily when he saw the mob. Their bright torches and weapons scared him. He stomped his feet. He groaned. Then he ran away from the village and into the country.

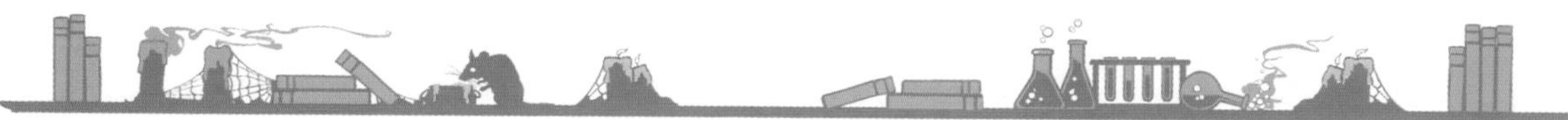

"Where did the monster go next?" asked Clerval.

"He ran until he found a place to hide," said Dr. Frankenstein.

The creature came upon a little cave in the country. He did not know why the villagers chased him away. He knew he should be where no one could see him. There, in his tiny cave, no one would be afraid of him.

But the monster was lonely. He moaned and groaned from loneliness. He discovered that he had neighbors. Their cottage was not far from his cave. He often watched them from the woods.

The monster saw that an old blind man lived in the cottage with his two children. The family was very poor. But they were very happy.

Sometimes, when the family left their cottage, the lonely monster would go inside. He borrowed books from their shelves. He taught himself how to read. He spent hours watching them and listening to them. He even taught himself how to speak. The monster loved to hear their voices. He also loved the sweet sound of the old man's guitar.

"Did they ever discover him?" asked Clerval.

"Yes, they did," said Dr. Frankenstein. "It was then that the poor monster's happiness ended."

"What happened to the family?" Clerval asked.

"Remember that the monster was still very young," said Dr. Frankenstein. "He was almost like a baby. He was still learning many new things."

Dr. Frankenstein sighed. "And the world was still not ready for him," the doctor said. Then the doctor told Clerval about the day that the monster met the poor family in the cottage.

One day, the children were not at home. The blind man was outside. The monster walked up to the blind man. They talked for a long time.

Then the children returned. Of course, their father was blind. He could not see the terrifying creature beside him. But the poor children could see the hideous monster. They were afraid. They screamed and shouted.

The creature tried to wave his arms to tell the children not to be afraid. The boy swung a log at the monster. When the girl screamed, the monster covered his ears and groaned.

The monster's deep voice and huge arms were unlike anything they had ever heard or seen before. The creature stomped his feet. He groaned. He was very upset. Then he gave up trying to calm the family down. He groaned and then ran away.

"What happened next?" Clerval asked.

"I was still looking for the monster," Dr. Frankenstein said. "I only wanted to find him. I wanted to help him."

"Help him?" Clerval asked. "But why?"

Dr. Frankenstein replied, "He sounded like he was kind and gentle. I wanted to give him a safe place to live."

"Did you ever find him?" Clerval asked.

Dr. Frankenstein sighed again. "No, I did not," he answered.

Dr. Frankenstein traveled all over the world. He talked to many people about the creature. He heard many horrifying stories about a strange creature.

The creature made terrible, deep noises. The creature crept through the woods. The creature stole food from fields. He peeked through windows at night. When people screamed, he groaned and ran away.

The monster ran far away from people.

The monster went through the snowy Alpine Mountains to the North Pole. Dr. Frankenstein followed the monster all the way to the North Pole. He hid there. It was a vast land covered with ice and snow. Dr. Frankenstein looked for the monster, but he could not find him.

"What happened next?" Clerval asked.

"I gave up," Dr. Frankenstein said. "I came home."

"Is the monster still alive?" Clerval asked.

"Probably not," the doctor said.

"What have I done?" Dr. Frankenstein shook his head and cried. "I gave the monster life, but it was a terrible life for the creature. People screamed wherever the monster went. He had to run away."

"Do you think the monster was angry with you?" Clerval asked.

"The monster must have been lonely and angry," Dr. Frankenstein said.

Clerval shook his head sadly. "Then, my friend, it is good that you never found the monster. He might be angry and looking for revenge."

"I doubt that I will ever see the monster again," said Dr. Frankenstein.

Just then, a bright bolt of lightning struck nearby. Dr. Frankenstein breathed in sharply at the alarming sound.

"The story of the monster was a terrible tale," Clerval said, "but now your long search is over."

Dr. Frankenstein said, "It's good to be home, where I'll be comfortable and safe again."

Bigfoot

Written by Brian Conway
Illustrated by Jason Wolff

One summer in 1966, Tim and Tanya Saunders went camping. In the woods, they saw many plants and animals they could not see in their neighborhood. They also saw something quite unusual.

Tim and Tanya were playing near their campsite. They saw something move in the trees. It was a giant, furry figure. It looked like it was watching them. Tim stepped closer to get a better look, but Tanya pulled him back.

Just then, the creature stepped out from behind a large tree. The brother and sister could see its huge arms and legs. Its whole body was covered with shaggy, brown fur. It stood on two feet, straight up and down like a human being. It sniffed the air and looked at them curiously with its big black eyes.

Tim and Tanya screamed and ran as fast as they could to find their mom and dad. When they returned with their parents, the creature was gone. All that was left was a single footprint.

It was a huge footprint, twice as big as Tim's or Tanya's footprint. It was not left there by a regular man. It was not like any animal's tracks either. Only a very large, very heavy creature could leave a footprint that big and deep.

What Tim and Tanya saw in the woods is called a Bigfoot. Many people have been searching for Bigfoot.

Nearly two thousand people have told stories like Tim and Tanya's. All of these people saw a furry giant that looked like an ape. The creature stood up like a human and walked on two feet.

Most of the reports about Bigfoot occurred in the woods of California, Oregon, Washington, and Canada. Some stories go as far back as Indian times. Long ago, the Salish Indians told stories about the "Sasquatch." This name means "wild man of the woods." But there is still no definite proof that the creature actually exists.

Many Bigfoot tracks have been found in the woods. The footprints look like human footprints, but are much larger and deeper. They are all around fourteen to eighteen inches long and five to seven inches wide.

Scientists say that any creature who made a footprint like that would be nearly eight feet tall and weigh up to eight hundred pounds!

Some people have gone to the woods to find a real Bigfoot. Some Bigfoot "hunters" brought photos back. Experts who looked at the photos cannot tell if the creatures in the photos are real or fake.

In 1967, Robert Patterson brought a movie camera to the woods. His famous film shows a female Bigfoot who is about seven feet tall and weighs about three hundred pounds.

Patterson's short film is the best evidence of a Bigfoot. Some scientists think the Bigfoot in the movie is a man dressed in a furry costume.

Many scientists who believe in Bigfoot think the creature is a relative of the caveman. It is halfway between a man and an ape. It looks like an ape but walks like a man.

These scientists say there is no reason to be afraid of Bigfoot. These creatures are shy and keep to themselves. That is why they live deep in the woods, away from people.

Many other scientists do not believe in Bigfoot. They say the photos and the footprints are not strong enough proof. They want to see bones or even a real Bigfoot! Until then, they will think Bigfoot is a myth, a story, or a legend.

Bigfoot stories are very real to people who have seen these creatures. Tim and Tanya Saunders, the boy and the girl who saw Bigfoot, think what they saw was real. People might think they made it up as a story. But Tim or Tanya will never forget the day they saw Bigfoot.

The Wreckers' Daughter

Written by Virginia R. Biles
Illustrated by Teresa Flavin

Chambercombe Manor was a very large house on the rocky coastline of Devonshire in England. For three hundred years it was haunted by the ghost of a young woman.

One owner after another reported seeing the young woman. No one ever reported being afraid of the ghost. But no one ever knew who she was—not for three hundred long years.

Then about one hundred years ago, the owner of the house discovered a tiny room. It had been hidden away behind plastered walls for years. Inside the little room was the skeleton of a young woman. She was lying on a beautiful bed. She was still dressed in the clothes she had worn more than two hundred years before.

The clothes had been soft and beautiful, but they were now dusty and fragile. The skeleton wore beautiful rings and necklaces, now dark with age.

But still, no one knew the woman's name. No one knew why she had been hidden away in the tiny room for so many years. The skeleton was soon buried in a small cemetery in the village. But the sad ghost continued to walk up and down the halls of the old house. Why was she there?

In the 1600's, Chambercombe Manor was owned by Thomas and Mary Oatway. The Oatways owned a little shop. But no one knew that the Oatways were wreckers.

During stormy weather, when the Oatways knew that a ship was sailing by the coastline, they would build a fire on the shore. The captain of the ship would think the fire was a light to guide him to safety. He would sail his ship into the big rocks on the coast.

The ship would crash into pieces. The cargo would wash up on the shore. The Oatways would gather all the valuable goods and store them in a cave. The cave led to a secret tunnel that went right into their house. No passengers or crew ever lived to tell the story.

One night long ago, the sky was black except for some streaks of lightning. Thomas searched the sea each time the lightning flashed.

"Aye, she's still there," he shouted. "Maybe she has seen our fire."

"Pile on more wood. We must make a large light for the ship to see," Mary said. "We need more goods for our store." Mary and Thomas piled more wood on the blazing fire so the heavy rain would not put it out.

"She's seen our fire," Thomas said. "She thinks it's the safe channel."

Mary and Thomas stood in the rain and wind. They watched the ship roll and toss on the waves. They heard the crunch of wood as the bow of the ship struck the rocks.

"There she is, Mary," Thomas yelled. "She's wrecked!"

Mary thought she heard cries for help above the roar of the waves. She closed her eyes and put her hands over her ears.

They began to search for the boxes and crates. Thomas set his lantern by his side to pick up the boxes. The yellow rays from the lantern fell on a still body lying face down in a shallow pool of water.

"There's a woman here," Thomas called. "I think she is alive."

They pulled the woman from the water. Thomas leaned down and put his ear to her heart.

"She is alive," he said.

Mary saw that the woman's face was badly cut from the jagged rocks. Her heart sank. She wanted to help this young woman. "We can't leave her here," she said to Thomas.

"All right, Mary, we'll take the lady with us," Thomas said. He picked up the woman and carried her safely into the cave.

Three days passed. Mary was pouring the tea when she heard a knock at the front door.

Mary crossed through the hall and swung open the heavy door. Before her stood a tall, well-dressed man. His head was bandaged. His arm was in a sling.

"Mrs. Mary Oatway?" he asked.

"Yes. I am Mary Oatway," Mary said.

"I am afraid I have very bad news for you," the stranger said. "May I please come in?"

Mary invited the stranger inside. They sat quietly and drank tea until the man broke the silence.

"Four days ago, I was on a ship from Ireland. But it sunk off your coast. I am the only survivor," he said.

Mary's face turned pale. Thomas gripped the arms of his chair. Did the man know that they had built the fire that caused the ship to wreck?

"I'm afraid I have some very bad news for you," he repeated. "Your daughter, Elizabeth, ran away to Ireland thirteen years ago. She had married a wealthy Irish gentleman. I met her on the ship that sunk. She missed you terribly and was coming to visit. It was supposed to be a surprise."

In the 1960's, construction workers were tearing down an old house in Ireland. They found a metal box. Inside the metal box was a letter addressed to the owners of Chambercombe Manor, Combe Martin, Devonshire, England. The letter read:

Before I die, I wish to confess my sins. My good wife is now dead. I cannot go unless someone knows what I have done. My wife and I lived for a number of years in Chambercombe Manor.

We were blessed with a beautiful daughter, who ran away when she was still a girl. We caused a ship to wreck and killed our own daughter in the wreck. We placed her body in a secret room. We could no longer live in our house. We thought we saw our daughter's ghost in the house. We moved to Ireland so we could be near our grandchildren.

May God forgive us.

Signed, Thomas Oatway

1690

The Inn at the End of the Lane

Written by Lora Kalkman
Illustrated by Teri Weidner

Erica folded her purple pajamas and put them in her suitcase. "There," she said. "I'm ready to go, Mom."

Erica and her mother were going on vacation. Mom had made plans for the them to visit Aunt Jill. Aunt Jill lived in a quaint little town near the ocean. Erica and her mother loved to visit the ocean.

The sky was a bit overcast as Erica and her mother turned onto the interstate. It was already late in the afternoon. Erica gazed out the window. The skyscrapers of the city soon gave way to trees and fields.

As they headed north, it started to rain. At first, big, fat droplets splashed slowly against the windshield.

Then, all of a sudden, the raindrops pounded fast and furiously. Mom turned the windshield wipers on as fast as they would go.

Just then, there was a loud crack of thunder. A bolt of lightning lit up the sky, which had grown quite dark.

"It's raining buckets," Mom declared. "I can hardly see to drive."

"Maybe we should pull over," Erica said.

Erica was scared. They were still several hours from Aunt Jill's house. Worse, they seemed to be stuck in the middle of nowhere.

"Look," Mom said, leaning forward and squinting. "There's an inn up ahead. Perhaps we could stay there tonight."

Erica felt relieved as they pulled up to a quaint farmhouse. It was white with green shutters. The house looked very inviting.

Erica and her mother grabbed their suitcases and rushed to the front porch. Thankfully, the porch was covered, providing shelter from the rain. Mom rang the doorbell. Before long, they heard footsteps in the hall.

"Welcome," said the innkeeper, as she opened the door. "Please come in and make yourselves at home."

"We'd like to rent a room for the evening," said Erica's mother. "I hope you still have one available."

"Certainly, dear," the lady said. "It is quite a storm we're having."

"It sure is!" Erica said.

The lady led the travelers to a cozy upstairs bedroom. Erica was pleased to see a giant bed with a fluffy comforter. As thunder boomed outside, she could hardly wait to snuggle under the warm, dry covers.

The next morning, Erica awoke to the sound of birds chirping. The terrible storm was over.

Erica and her mother walked downstairs. The parlor looked even lovelier in the bright light of morning.

"Hello?" Erica's mother called out.

Erica and her mother could not find the innkeeper.

Erica's mother shrugged her shoulders. "Maybe she went out for groceries," she said. "We can just leave a note."

Erica's mother rummaged through her purse for some paper. She neatly wrapped a note around some money and placed them on the table in the hall.

After driving a few miles, they stopped to get gas.

"Can I help you?" the boy at the gas station asked pleasantly.

"We'd like a fill-up," Erica's mom replied.

"Sure thing," the boy said. He placed the nozzle into the gas tank.

"You didn't happen to drive through that terrible storm last night, did you?" the boy continued.

"As a matter of fact, we did," Erica's mom said. "Fortunately, we were able to spend the night at that charming inn a few miles back."

The boy turned and looked at them. "You don't mean the white farmhouse with the green shutters?" he asked, looking puzzled.

"Why, yes!" Erica's mother replied. "The hostess was so kind."

"But that's impossible," the boy said slowly. "That's Mrs. Flattery's old inn. It burned down several days ago."

"Burned down?" Erica repeated in surprise.

Erica's mother figured the boy was joking. She waited for him to laugh. But he seemed very serious. Erica had a creepy feeling.

"Let's drive back, Mom," she suggested. "It will only take a few minutes."

Erica held her breath as they approached the inn. When they pulled into the drive, she could hardly believe their eyes! Sure enough, the old house was burned, just like the boy had said.

"How can that be?" Erica stammered in disbelief. "We were just here!"

The porch that had protected them from the rain was now sagging and burned. The windows were all broken.

Carefully, Erica made her way to the opening where the front door used to be. Then she gasped. There before her was the hall table. And on it was their neatly folded note.

The Banshee and O'Doud

Written by Lynne Suesse
Illustrated by Frank Sofo

Aiken O'Doud was a man of few beliefs. He did not believe in leprechauns. He did not believe in fairies. He did not believe in Santa Claus!

"Only silly children believe in such things," he would say. The only thing Aiken O'Doud believed was that he knew everything.

Aiken O'Doud was a reporter for a very important newspaper. The name of the newspaper was *The Truth.* Aiken O'Doud thought that this was the best name for a paper. "I do not believe in anything but the truth," he told his boss one day.

Aiken O'Doud's boss would send him to different places to write stories.

"I have a great story for you," his boss said one day. He told Aiken to go to the Irish village of Limerick. "I want you to write a story about the banshee," he said.

"I don't believe in banshees!" O'Doud said.

But the next day, Aiken O'Doud packed a bag and made sure that he had his notebook. He bought a train ticket for the village of Limerick.

"I'm going to write the story, but I will not believe in banshees," O'Doud grumbled to himself.

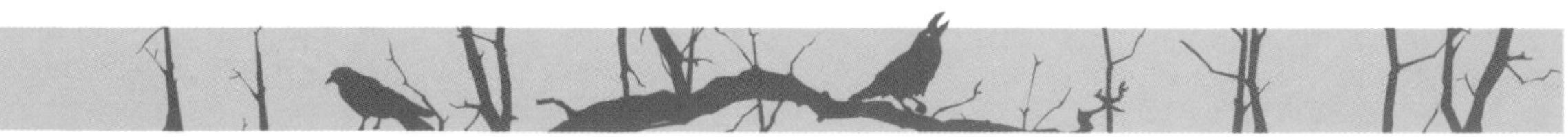

Aiken O'Doud grumbled to himself the whole train ride. "Banshees? Ha!" he would say. Passengers seated around O'Doud moved away. O'Doud did not care. He grumbled to himself even louder.

O'Doud arrived in Limerick. He grumbled to himself as he walked to the Cloverleaf Inn.

O'Doud got right to work and began to ask questions about the banshee. The innkeeper told O'Doud how the banshee took the life of an old woman on the edge of the village.

"An old woman?" asked O'Doud. "How do you know that the banshee had anything to do with it?"

The innkeeper told O'Doud the villagers had heard screaming. "It was the howling of the banshee!" cried the innkeeper. "We all heard it just before the old woman fell."

"I don't believe such a thing," said O'Doud. "It must have been the wind."

"The wind indeed," said the innkeeper. He did not like O'Doud. "Go ask the other villagers. They will tell you what they heard."

"I'll do just that!" said O'Doud. O'Doud became angry that his boss sent him to this village. He thought the banshee story was silly.

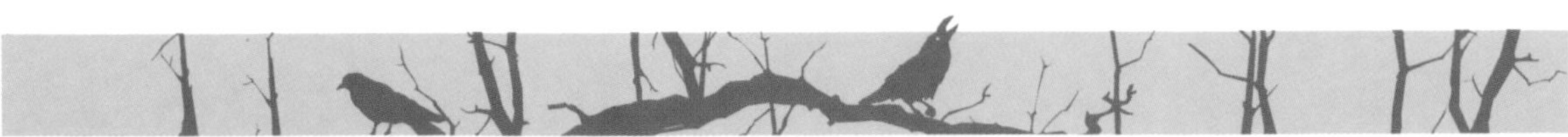

Even though O'Doud did not believe in banshees, he wanted to learn more about the old woman. "Nobody can say that I did not do my job," said O'Doud. He went to visit the old woman's neighbors at the edge of the village.

Timmy O'Daley lived next door to the old woman. He was very excited to talk to O'Doud. "I have never really talked to a reporter before," Timmy said.

Timmy told O'Doud about the screaming he had heard the day the old woman disappeared. "It scared my cat right up the chimney, it did!" he said.

"Are you sure you didn't just hear the wind?" asked O'Doud.

"I never heard the wind sound like that before!" said Timmy.

"Are you sure?" O'Doud asked.

Timmy went on to tell O'Doud about the legend of the banshee. "She's a fierce spirit, the banshee is," said Timmy. "Nobody sees her. But you know she is coming when you hear her scream. But her victim never hears the scream. So if everyone around you hears screaming and you don't, you're in trouble."

"She screams, you say," said O'Doud, making a note.

"When she screams, something bad is going to happen," said Timmy.

"Something bad. Yes, I see. Thank you for your time," said O'Doud. He wrote what Timmy said in his notebook, but he did not believe him.

"These people are crazy," thought O'Doud. "Next they're going to tell me that a leprechaun has left a pot of gold at the end of a rainbow!"

O'Doud left Timmy O'Daley. He walked back into the village. O'Doud knew he needed some more information for his newspaper story. He went to visit the local shopkeepers.

As O'Doud walked through the village, people stopped talking to each other. They tipped their hats or nodded politely.

O'Doud stopped to talk to Minnie O'Connell. Minnie ran the bakery. She was talking to Mrs. O'Malley.

"The banshee does not like those who don't believe," Mrs. O'Malley said.

"How do you know the banshee is real?" O'Doud asked.

"The banshee is real, you know," said Minnie. "You city folk think you've seen it all. But you've never seen or heard anything like the banshee."

O'Doud stopped writing for a moment. He looked up at Minnie.

"The likes of you better be careful," said Mrs. O'Malley.

O'Doud scribbled in his notebook and laughed to himself. He thought the women were trying to scare him. It did not work. O'Doud went back to the Cloverleaf Inn to sleep.

O'Doud woke up to a new day. He did not want to talk to more villagers. O'Doud thought the people in the village did not like him. He did not care. He thought that they were silly people with silly beliefs.

O'Doud got dressed and walked down the street. He was looking for a good place to eat breakfast. The villagers said hello. O'Doud thought he heard them say, "Good morning, O'Doubt!" He thought they were laughing.

"It must be my imagination," O'Doud said to himself.

O'Doud found a restaurant and asked the waiter for a cup of coffee.

"Did you hear the screaming last night?" the waiter asked, as he put a cup of hot coffee on the table.

O'Doud took a sip of the coffee. He did not hear any screaming last night.

"It kept me up," said the waiter. "All that strange screaming. It sounded just like the scream I heard right before the old woman disappeared."

"I'm sure it was the wind," said O'Doud.

The waiter bent down close to O'Doud and said, "Did you hear any wind last night, O'Doubt?"

O'Doud tried to eat his breakfast, but all the villagers stopped by to talk about the banshee.

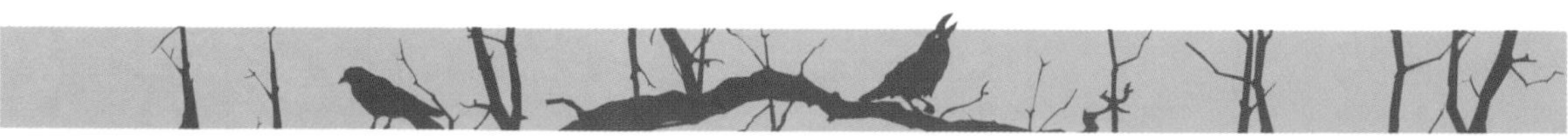

O'Doud finished eating. Then he paid the waiter and left the restaurant.

O'Doud could not forget what the waiter had said. He thought about the screaming that people had heard in the night. He wondered why he had not heard all the noise.

As he walked near the village square, O'Doud looked at all the people. He saw Timmy O'Daley and Minnie O'Connell. He thought that they looked funny. He saw them looking around.

Then O'Doud saw that all the people had strange looks on their faces. He saw a few people cover their ears, as if they heard a loud sound.

"I think your wind is back again," shouted Timmy. Timmy covered his ears.

O'Doud did not hear anything. He looked around and around. He felt dizzy. He could not breathe.

Suddenly, O'Doud was struck down by the banshee!

The people of Limerick gathered around the man that they had all called "O'Doubt." The pages of his notebook blew in the wind.

Then a leprechaun peeked out from behind a stone and said, "Is O'Doubt gone then?"

Indeed, he is.

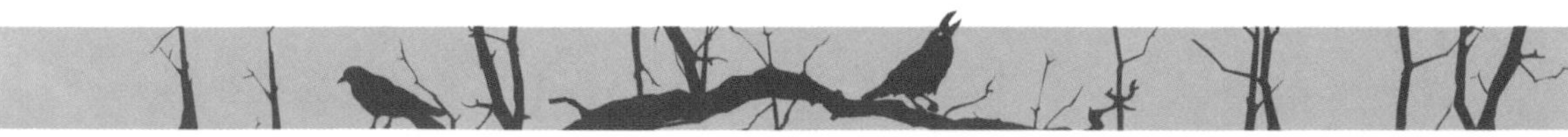

The Second Captain

Written by Lisa Harkrader
Illustrated by Jo Ellen Bosson

Robert's breath came out in white puffs as he spoke. "That should be the last of all the cargo, Captain," he said. "We should be right on schedule."

Captain Connor nodded. "Good. We don't need any delays."

Robert and the captain stood on the pier, watching their crew load the remaining crates into the hull of the long freighter. Icy wind whipped in from the ocean and whistled across the wooden planks below Robert's feet. Robert huddled down in his jacket and licked the salty mist from his lips.

Robert was the ship's first mate, the captain's right hand man. But this was his first trip to Newfoundland, and he wanted to be prepared.

"Do you think we'll run into any problems, sir?" he said.

The captain gazed out across the choppy gray water. "I've made this voyage many times, Robert. No two journeys are the same. This time of year, we'll have to remain alert. We can't let our guard down. Icebergs flow down from the north. Our ship is sturdy, but it would shatter against an iceberg. You need to be ready for icebergs."

"I will, sir," said Robert. "I'll be ready."

Robert and Captain Connor boarded the ship. They climbed to the bridge and settled into their desks. The captain recorded their departure in the ship's logbook while Robert began his navigational calculations.

After about an hour, the captain stood up and stretched. "Robert, I need to go below to chart the ship's position," he said. "I am leaving you in charge of the bridge."

The ship was far out at sea. Their best helmsman, O'Brien, was at the wheel. Robert had nearly finished his navigational calculations.

Robert set back to work and finished the calculations. Now all he had to do was ask the captain for the ship's position.

Robert set down his instruments and rubbed his eyes. When he looked up, he was startled to see Captain Connor had returned to the bridge. The captain was at his desk, scrawling in the ship's logbook.

Robert picked up his instruments and studied his calculations.

"Can you confirm the ship's position, sir?" Robert asked.

The captain did not answer.

"Captain?" asked Robert, still glancing through his calculations. "Can you confirm the ship's position?"

Again the captain did not answer.

Robert looked up. The captain's desk was empty. The captain was gone.

"That's odd." Robert frowned. "O'Brien, did you see the captain sitting at his desk just now?"

The helmsman shook his head. "No. The sea's too rough. I haven't taken my eyes off it."

Robert scratched his head. "The captain didn't say anything when he came in, he didn't say anything when I spoke to him, and he didn't say anything when he left. That's just not like him. He must be worried about something."

Robert left his desk and walked across the bridge to where the captain had been sitting. The logbook was still open on the captain's desk. Robert read the latest entry:

Change position immediately.

Tack northwest ten degrees.

Robert stared at the captain's words. "Ten degrees? That changes our course completely. Why didn't he say something?"

He turned to O'Brien. "Tack northwest ten degrees. Immediately. I'll go find the captain."

Robert looked all over the ship. Finally, he looked in the infirmary. He was surprised to see the captain there. A bandage covered the captain's head.

"Captain! Thank goodness I found you," said Robert. "I changed course as you requested."

The captain frowned. "As I requested?"

"Yes, sir," said Robert. "I saw your note in the ship's log. I ordered O'Brien to tack ten degrees northwest."

The captain stared at Robert. "I recorded nothing in the log," he said. "And I didn't go back up to the bridge. I hit my head when I was climbing down the ladder to the chart room."

Now it was Robert's turn to stare. "Sir, I saw you. I saw you at your desk. I saw what you wrote in the log." He stopped. "The log! Captain, I can prove what I'm saying. I'll be right back."

Robert raced from the infirmary and climbed the ladder to the bridge.

The warning bell sounded—*CLANG-CLANG! CLANG-CLANG!*

Robert bounded towards it. He ran even faster. He saw O'Brien leaning on the wheel. He was steering the ship away from an iceberg that loomed above the port deck.

"Thank goodness the captain ordered us to change course when he did," said O'Brien. "We would've hit her head-on."

Robert watched as the ship slipped past the ice. It was so close, Robert could nearly reach out and touch it.

When there was no more danger, Robert snatched the ship's logbook from the captain's desk and hurried back down to the infirmary.

"There, sir," Robert pointed at the last entry in the logbook. "Isn't that your handwriting?"

The captain studied the book. "It's my handwriting, all right, but I never wrote this!"

The captain sat straight up in bed. "My dream! I had a dream. In my dream I saw an iceberg. The ship was headed towards it. I knew we were going to hit it. I tried to tell you, Robert. I wanted you to change course, but I just could not get your attention."

Robert stared at him. "And in your dream, Captain, when you couldn't get my attention, what did you do?"

The captain's face went white. "I did the only thing I could do," he said. "I wrote 'tack ten degrees northwest' in the logbook."

The Little Room

Written by Leslie Lindecker
Illustrated by Nan Brooks

Maria and Claudia climbed the steps to their train car. The sisters had flown to Montpelier. Now they were taking a train on the Central Vermont Railway. They were traveling to see their aunts who lived in a very old house near Highgate Springs.

"I am glad we will finally put an end to our disagreement," said Maria.

"So am I," agreed Claudia. "Let's hope our aunts will let us see the room."

As the train rumbled along by the Winsooki River, Maria and Claudia talked about their childhood visits with their aunts.

"Whenever I went by the little door off the kitchen, I saw bright sunshine under the door," said Maria. "One day, I quietly opened the door. The room was filled with sunshine. There was a big window. The furniture was brightly painted. There were shells everywhere."

"Did you go inside?" Claudia asked.

"I tried," Maria said. "I opened the door once. But Aunt Bedelia saw me and cried, 'Come away from there this instant!' I never was brave enough to open that door again."

"I remember the room," Claudia said. "It was not at all as you saw it, Maria. When I was little, the door off the kitchen always had a cool breeze blowing under it. I could smell flowers in the breeze. One day, I opened the door. The room was cool and dark. Red velvet curtains covered the window. The walls were covered with beautiful wallpaper. There were vases of deep red roses. The roses were the flowers I could smell when the breeze came under the door."

"Did you ever step inside the room?" Maria asked.

Claudia shook her head. "I tried, too. But Aunt Magnolia came up behind me and cried, 'Come away from there this instant!' I was never brave enough to open the door again," she said.

"Isn't it strange? We remember the room so differently," Maria said.

"I wonder why Aunt Bedelia and Aunt Magnolia did not want us to go into the room," Claudia said.

"It's quite a mystery," Maria answered.

The train clacked and creaked along the tracks.

"It will be good to see Aunt Bedelia and Aunt Magnolia again," Claudia said.

"I wonder if they have changed much since we last saw them," Maria said.

"I just hope they will finally let us see the room," Claudia said.

Maria and Claudia took a taxi to the old house where their aunts lived. The aunts were standing on the front porch when they arrived. The girls ran to the porch and hugged their aunts.

Maria said, "We hope you can solve a mystery for us. Both of us remember a little door off of the kitchen. I remember a room full of bright sunlight and seashells. Claudia remembers a room full of cool breezes, shadows, and roses. Who is right?"

The aunts looked at each other. Aunt Bedelia said, "Perhaps you are old enough to understand. Magnolia, please get the lamp."

Aunt Magnolia stood up. She picked up an oil lamp from the table.

Aunt Bedelia said, "The room you remember does not have shells in it. It does not have roses in it. Come and have a look."

The two young ladies followed their aunts to the little door off the kitchen. Aunt Magnolia held the lamp. Aunt Bedelia unlocked the door.

Claudia and Maria saw the stairs to the cellar. In the center of the cellar was a wooden marker that read:

Shelly and Rose

December 31, 1948

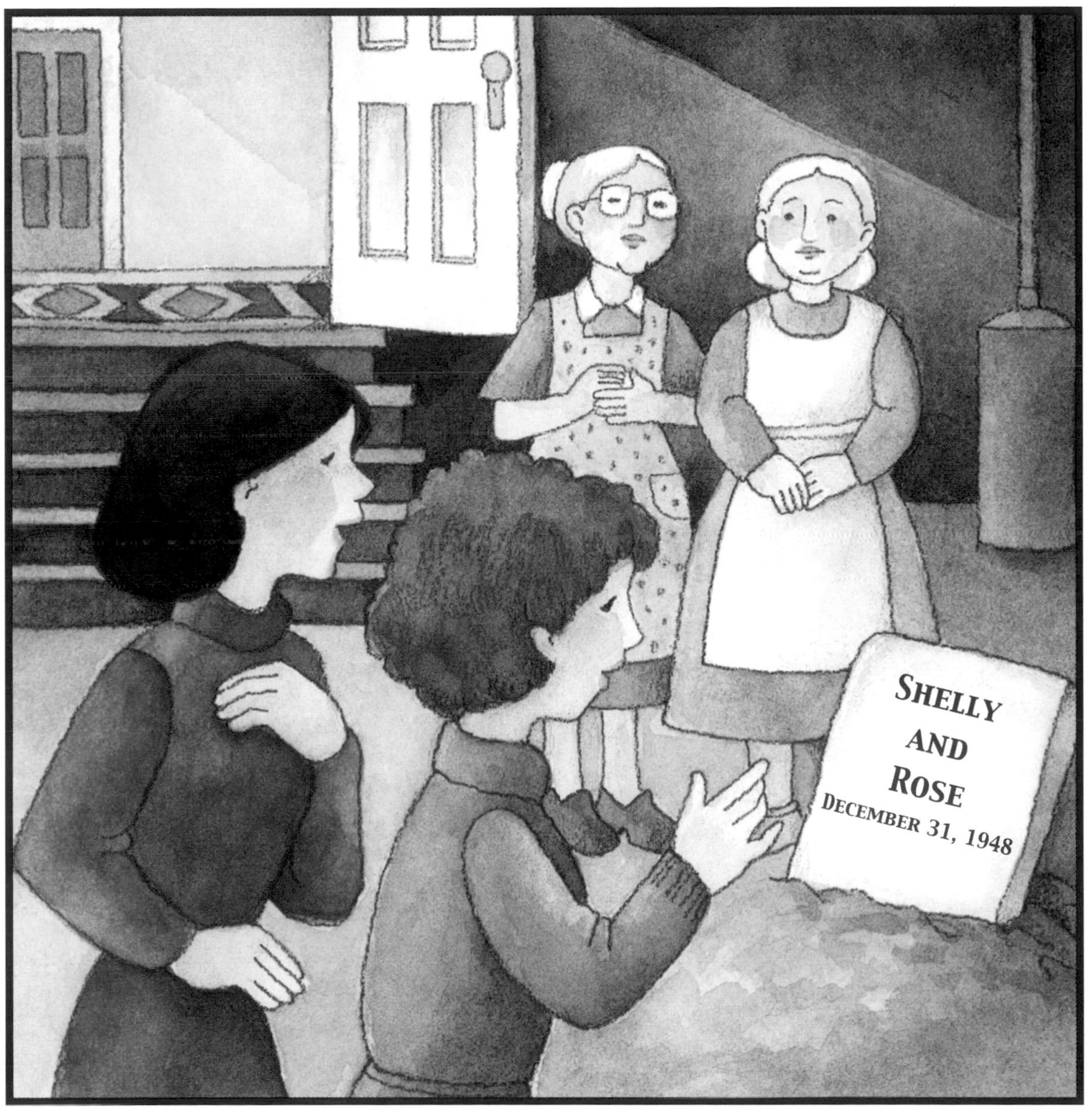
SHELLY
AND
ROSE
DECEMBER 31, 1948

Maria and Claudia stared at the marker.

"One winter night," Aunt Bedelia began, "when your Aunt Magnolia and I were only a little older than you are now, there was a terrible snowstorm. We heard a knock at the door. It was a young woman. She had a little baby that was wrapped in a shawl."

Aunt Magnolia continued the story. "We took the young woman and her baby in. She was almost frozen from the storm. We bundled them into bed with extra blankets. We built up the fire to make the room warmer. We fed them hot soup. We did our best to take care of the young woman and her baby. When morning came, both the baby and the young woman had died in their sleep."

Aunt Bedelia said, "We did not know what to do. It was winter and the ground outside was frozen. We had to bury them in the cellar. The ground was softer because it was warmed by the house. The young woman had a note in her hand. The note said, 'Take care of my Rose—Shelly.'"

Aunt Magnolia shook her head and said, "Some days this is just our cellar with a wooden marker in the center of it. On other days, it is a room filled with sunshine and seashells."

"Other days, it is a room filled with roses and shadows," said Aunt Bedelia.

"Did you ever find out who they were?" Claudia asked.

Aunt Bedelia answered, "We could not find anyone who knew the young woman. All we had was the note she was holding in her hand."

Aunt Magnolia said, "I think the young woman knew we tried to help her. Whenever the room appears, there is a happy feeling in it."

"If the room is sunny and bright, you feel like dancing and singing. If the room is filled with roses, you feel peaceful," said Aunt Bedelia.

Maria, Claudia, Aunt Bedelia, and Aunt Magnolia walked back up the stairs.

"I did not know your house was haunted. That would have scared me when I was little," Maria said.

"That is why we did not want you to go into the room," Aunt Bedelia said.

"We did not want you to be frightened," Aunt Magnolia said.

As the young women and their aunts stepped back into the kitchen, the steps began to fade.

If they had looked back, they would have seen that the room was bright and sunny. There were many seashells scattered about. There were vases of deep red roses on the tabletops. A young woman sat in a rocking chair and sang softly to a sweet little baby.

Ghost Hunters

Written by Brian Conway
Illustrated by Cheryl Kirk Noll

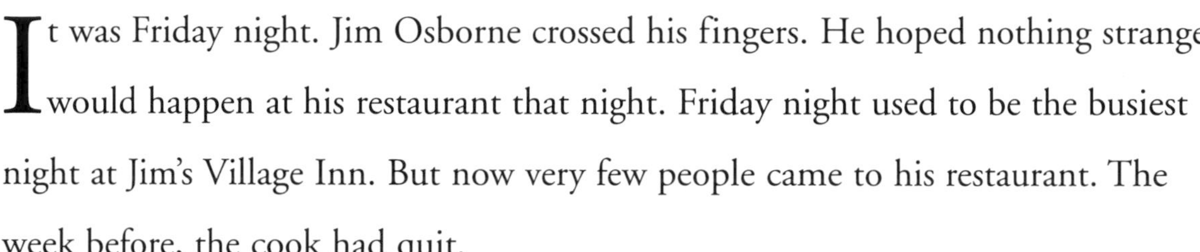

It was Friday night. Jim Osborne crossed his fingers. He hoped nothing strange would happen at his restaurant that night. Friday night used to be the busiest night at Jim's Village Inn. But now very few people came to his restaurant. The week before, the cook had quit.

"How can I get the food ready?" the cook had asked. "The flame on the stove keeps blowing out! Food is missing from the cupboard! Every time I turn around, the freezer door opens! I can't stand it!"

Word was spreading around town that Jim's Village Inn was haunted.

Jim watched as a family started to eat their dinner. The table shook and their plates crashed to the floor. Jim went to apologize for the mess. The family was shocked. They wanted an explanation. But Jim did not have one.

Jim picked up the phone. He dialed a number from a newspaper ad.

"Incident Investigations," a voice answered.

"This is Jim Osborne," Jim said. "I run Jim's Village Inn. I need your help."

"Close your restaurant early tonight," said the ghost hunter. "I will be there before midnight."

Ghost hunters do their best work at night. They study poltergeists. Poltergeists are ghosts that knock things over. They make a lot of noise.

Ghost hunters do not study every case they hear about. Some events can be easily explained. Sometimes people are just imagining things.

But some cases are truly unusual. These cases demand an expert and that is when the ghost hunter comes to investigate.

In their investigations, ghost hunters use the tools of science. A ghost hunter's kit would contain a camera, a sound recorder, and a thermometer.

Harry Price was a famous ghost hunter. He studied hundreds of haunted places. He did not believe a place was haunted until he could find scientific proof.

Price wanted to get evidence that he could record. He studied a haunted place by spending the night in it. Price wanted to record sounds and watch for movement.

He spread flour on the floor to detect footprints. He set up motion-sensitive alarms that would wake him up.

Sometimes tables shook, lamps fell over, or doors locked. There was nobody in the house but Harry Price, and he had not moved. These were places that Harry Price proved were haunted.

Other famous ghost hunters were some of history's most respected scientists. They started out wanting to prove that haunts were just silly stories. But their studies changed their minds.

Sir William Crookes studied haunted houses in England during the 1800's. He attended many séances, when people get together to try to talk to spirits. He saw and heard many things that science could not explain.

Today's ghost hunters have advanced machines. They are used to sense the slightest changes in temperature or movements in the air. Machines can help the ghost hunters see in the dark. They also help to give proof that other people can see and believe.

Ghost hunters do not really "hunt" ghosts. There is nothing they can do to make ghosts go away. They hunt for proof in haunted places. Once they record ghostly activities or find no proof, their job is done.

Their work proves that ghosts are hard to track and impossible to trap. For these real-life ghost busters, the hunt continues.

A ghost hunter proved that Jim's Village Inn was inhabited by mischievous spirits. It is now called Jim's Haunted Inn. Every Friday night, people come from miles around to dine in the presence of a poltergeist.

The End